Diana Carter
P.O. Box 300795
Waterford, MI 48330
248-872-3015
diana.carter44@gmail.com

I0593876

IN THE NAME OF JUSTICE: THE ERICA BLACKSTONE

CHRONICLES

By

Diana Carter

OTHER BOOKS BY DIANA CARTER

BROKEN PROMISES SERIES

BROKEN PROMISES: SHATTERED DREAMS

BROKEN PROMISES: WHEN SHATTERED DREAMS BECOME REALITY

BROKEN PROMISES: SHATTERED DREAMS THE FINAL CHAPTER

DARK REVENGE: THE TREY TAYLOR STORY

In The Name of Justice: The Erica Blackstone Chronicles

General Fiction: Family/Relationship

All Rights Reserved

Copyright © 2017 by Diana Carter

This book is a work of fiction. Names, characters, places, and incidents are the product of the author's imagination or are used fictitiously. Any resemblance to actual events, locales, or persons, living or dead, is coincidental.

This book may not be reproduced, transmitted, or stored in whole or in part by any means, including graphic, electronic, or mechanical without the express written consent of the publisher except in the case of brief quotations embodied in critical articles and reviews.

LET'S DO THIS PUBLISHING, LLC
P.O. Box 300795
Waterford, MI 48330

ISBN 13: 978-0-9997106-0-9

Cover Designed by Professional Instant Printing. All Rights Reserved

PRINTED IN THE UNITED STATES OF AMERICA

Dedicated

The dedication of this book is to two very special teens in my life, my granddaughters Jimeeka Carter and Angel Woods. Jimeeka is my oldest grandchild. She graduated from high school and will be attending Oakland Community College. I'm so very proud of the accomplishments she's made in her life. The old saying is true, 'It's not how you start off, its how you finish.' Angel is special because she inspired me to do this spin-off to the *Broken Promises* series. I thought I was done with the series, but after receiving Angel's feedback that the Erica character needed her own story, I decided to extend the series. Since the Erica character played an important role in book three, I had to agree with Angel. As always, God is my main inspiration that gives me the courage to follow my dream of becoming a successful bestselling author. Without His guiding force, none of this would be possible.

Acknowledgements

It is my greatest wish that my loyal and faithful readers enjoy this spin-off to the **Broken Promises** series. Coming back to write this book was a little difficult after writing *Dark Revenge: The Trey Taylor Story,* but rewarding. After writing and publishing these two titles, it's time to get back to the roots of my writing: family drama. With that being said, the next titles to be published are titles in the four-book series: **The Sister Factor**. I intended to write and publish *The Candidate* before publishing this series, but a delay in completing *The Candidate* along with the completion of **The Sister Factor** series will place them in publication next.

I would like to acknowledge some special people that have given me constructive feedback after reading the **Broken Promises** series. To my co-worker Catherine McFarland, your feedback provided food for thought. I appreciate your open and honest opinion about the characters and the improvement of my writing. To my younger brother Danny Williams, I would like to thank you for giving me a male perspective on all three books, especially the last book in the series. To my baby sister Teresa Williams, as always your support is immeasurable. Finally,

I would like to thank Sarah Abraham, who not only read every book I've written, but also was the reason why I had the courage to move forward to fulfilling my dream of becoming a successful writer.

God's blessing,

Diana Carter

Chapter One

Erica and JJ sat in the conference room of their new office space reviewing the biggest case they've had since forming their partnership a year ago. Erica's aunt Arlene had been kind enough to lease them an entire floor in her building. Arlene refused to let them pay a normal rate for the space on the guise that the building was safer with the presence of a security company. While the usual case load for Jefferson & Blackstone Investigations (JBI) consisted of: backgrounds checks, civil investigations, fraud, accidental deaths, and infidelity, this new case was a child custody case that had been going on for months when the father decided it was time to hire outside help.

The client, Benjamin Joseph Bailey, was seeking sole custody of his two children Benjamin Jr. and Briana, stating that his wife, Nina was unfit because of her mental instability. Benjamin was the president of First National Bank. His long hours at work were the basis of Nina's countersuit claims. She insisted Benjamin didn't even know their children, attend any of their activities, or spend quality time with them.

Because of JJ's personal friendship with the new client, Erica wanted to be certain there was no conflict of interest in taking the case. Erica enjoyed working with JJ. The two of them had connected years ago when they worked on Arlene's hit-and-run and Emily's (Erica's mom) abduction. They made a great team, but Erica was a little worried about their new case. JJ had recently returned to work after four weeks of maternity leave and wouldn't be able to handle her normal workload. Erica knew it had to be hard for JJ to leave her one-month old son Leonard Jeffrey Wheeler (Leo for short). Between her heart for her friend and her postpartum hormones, would JJ be objective enough to keep her head on the case? Erica wasn't sure.

"Okay, Erica, what do you think we should do about this case?" JJ asked. "You will be handling most of the caseload, so I don't want to take it on if you're not up to it right now."

"Well, it's something out of the ordinary for us and could be great for future business. But I do think we should look at all the angles before we make a commitment."

"I know. The only reason I said we would look over the case is because of the relationship we have with the bank. They were one of my most steady clients in the early days of business, but I don't want my personal friendship with Ben to be a deciding factor."

"How well do you know Ben? He seems like a likable fellow, but some of the issues in this case look like they could get real ugly."

"I know him well enough to know he's a good dad, but I'll be the first to admit he's been married to his career for a long time, and his wife is right that he hasn't been present for most of the children's lives."

"What about his wife? What's the deal with her?"

"She's a piece of work. I don't like her personally, but I don't want that to get in the way of her losing her children if she really cares about their safety and well-being."

"I know what you mean. I remember when all that stuff happened with Auntie Delores, and I kind of took her side. My family lost their mind. I don't want to be put in a position like that ever again. I hurt my mom and aunties so much. Sometimes I think they're still a little disappointed in my actions."

9

"Erica, you know your family doesn't have any bad feelings towards you for speaking what was on your heart at the time. They love and respect you for standing up for what you believed, even if it was different than what they were feeling."

"I know, but I hope that is the last time I ever have to be on the other side of them. They are very intimidating to go up against when they get their mind fixed on something they feel is wrong."

"Speaking of your mom how does she like having all of her grandchildren living in Michigan now?"

"She is ecstatic. So are my aunties and uncles. It took a while for the twins to adjust. They were so used to getting all the attention in the family, sharing was a little hard for them at first."

"I still can't believe it's been two years since all of that went down with your family." JJ shook her head. "I will always have feelings for Eric, but giving my relationship a second chance with Lewis was the best decision I've ever made." Her face broke into a wide grin.

Erica was happy things weren't so tense any more between JJ and her Uncle Eric. "Two years ago, my mom was abducted and my Aunt

Arlene involved in a hit and run. My brother, Calvin relocated from Washington to help us solve both cases and decided to relocate the family here." Erica sighed, "I'm happy things aren't so tense between you and Uncle Eric anymore, but I love the way your face lights up at the thought of Lewis." Lewis Wheeler was the longtime assistant of Emily.

JJ laughed. "Lewis is so good with Leo…" JJ continued doting on her family. "It was harder for him to go back to work than it was for me to come back here." JJ's eyes were misty. Erica squeezed her hand. JJ was at peace that both she and Eric were now happily married to other people.

"We could talk about my cute godson and our families all day I'm sure, but I think we've gotten a little off track. Let's review this case and see if we're going to take it so we can get with Ben later today." Returning to work mode the ladies spent the rest of the morning working what may be one of their most controversial cases. With Nina coming from a well-connected family, the case had the potential to draw national attention. Erica wanted to be certain they were ready.

On the other side of town Benjamin and Nina Bailey sat in their pastor's office in yet another session that seemed to be going nowhere. This was their fourth session with Pastor Collins since the couple decided to divorce more than four months ago. After praying with the couple, the pastor sat and observed their interactions with each other. He was saddened by what he saw. Years ago, the Baileys had been so in love. He was sure they would be a forever couple. Now the tension was so thick in the room Pastor Collins felt the need to break up the dismal silence.

"How have the two of you been since we last met?"

Benjamin surprised the pastor by responding first.

"Pastor Collins, I would like to thank you for taking the time to have these private sessions with us, but this isn't working. Our marriage is damaged beyond repair, and I think it's time to cut our losses and move on."

"You see, Pastor. This is what I've been saying all along. He's a quitter." Pastor Collins was surprised by the anger in Nina's voice.

"I'm not a quitter. I just know when it's time to cut my losses. You are so hateful it's affecting our children."

"Please, don't act like you give a damn about our children. When was the last time you made it to any of their activities or school functions?"

"Pastor, I'm in the process of delegating some of my duties so I can be more accessible to my children. All I care about is their well-being and if I don't get them away from their mom, she will ruin them for life."

"You are not taking my children anywhere. You can hire all the private investigators you want, but that isn't going to change the fact that you're not getting your hands on my children." Benjamin's eyes widened.

"You thought you were one step ahead of me, but I have eyes everywhere so you better watch your step." Nina smirked at Benjamin.

"Let's tone this conversation down a notch. Nina, I heard from Benjamin on the status of your marriage. What is your take on how things

13

are working out between you guys?" Pastor Collins wanted to try to get the couple back to a more even ground.

"I feel the same way as this fool. He's been absent from this marriage for a long time. I'm sick of trying to save the family all by myself."

"Save the family. Woman, you need to come back to reality. You've been cheating on me for years and Lord knows what else you've been doing."

"That isn't true. We should be talking about this in private." The Pastor could see that Nina was about to explode.

"There's nothing else to be said. You told me you didn't want the children so I don't know why you're fighting me for custody. I'm fed up with you Nina."

"You know I didn't mean to say that. You were getting on my last nerve, at the time, and I just wanted you to leave me the hell alone." Nina was finding it hard to hold in her anger.

"Nina, please stop this mess. Take some time to get into treatment and get your life back together and maybe in the future after things are better for you, we can discuss joint custody."

"You ARE NOT getting my children. Pastor, I'm sorry but this isn't working for me. I need to get out of here." Nina stood and left the Pastor's office. Benjamin nodded at Pastor Collins and shook his hand, then followed Nina.

Chapter Two

Erica intentionally arrived at work early Monday morning to have some time alone before the others arrived. She didn't expect JJ until the afternoon because she had to take Leo to his first doctor's appointment. The weekend went by fast, but she was able to get a handle on Benjamin's case. After talking it over with JJ and her brother Calvin, (their legal counsel for JBI), they decided to go ahead and take the case. Erica drifted through memories of the last few years, thinking about the time she donated her bone marrow to save her cousin DJ's life and her uncle Eric, and auntie Delores' speedy wedding. Knock. Knock. Erica tucked her thoughts away and went to open the door. Seeing her brother Calvin's smiling face made her day.

"Hello, big brother. I didn't expect to see you today."

"Well, if you don't mind, I'd like to sit in on the meeting today with Benjamin."

"Sure, but that's not until two o'clock."

"What time do you think it is, baby girl?" Erica looked at her watch and was shocked to see it was nearly one thirty.

"Oh my God, I didn't get any work done this morning."

"What were you doing?"

"I was thinking about some of the things that happened in our family since we met DJ."

"Wow you went way back in the past. What made you reminisce about the old days?"

"Partially the case, I'm having mixed feelings about taking it on. I know Ben is a good friend of JJ's, but something isn't sitting right with me about the entire thing."

"I know the feeling. That's why I wanted to be in on it from the beginning. His soon to be ex-wife is reminding me of Clarissa and Jessica, and that's not a good thing." Clarissa was the mother of Arlene's young lover David Redmond Jr., and Jessica was Eric's high school sweetheart that he married later in life and was partially responsible for Arlene's hit-and-run a few years back. They both tended to over escalate issues and create a lot of drama.

"I was thinking the same thing. I just don't want to disappoint JJ. She speaks highly of Ben and says that he's a good guy stuck in a bad situation."

"Be that as it may, you guys have to be careful dealing with a mother threatened with the loss of her children."

Before Erica could respond, JJ walked in the door with a big smile on her face.

"Look at the new mom." Calvin gushed.

"Hi, cutie pie, you know I'm just saying that in fun because I'm happily married to the man I should have married years ago."

Calvin laughed and shook his head. "I know, JJ. I'm happy everything is working out for you. Now the case, I'm a little concerned about. I was just telling Erica that I'm sensing Nina may be as volatile as Clarissa and Jessica, and I don't want either of you put in harm's way."

"I feel you, Calvin but I don't think Nina is dangerous just self-centered. Why don't we wait and see how the meeting goes? Then we'll have a better feel for what we're getting into." Erica and Calvin nodded in agreement and the trio made small talk while they waited for Benjamin to arrive.

Arlene and Emily were in Arlene's office having their afternoon tea while Erica, JJ, and Calvin was downstairs meeting with Benjamin Bailey. They were discussing among other things how peaceful things have been for the last few years and how happy everyone in the family was in their lives. The last thing they needed was any drama of a dangerous nature.

"Lennie, I don't like the fact that Benjamin's wife seems unstable."

"I know what you mean, Em. We had enough crazy in the family to last us a lifetime. But, I'm sure Erica and JJ will be able to handle the situation, especially since Calvin has offered to assist them on the case."

"I guess not having any drama in the family for the last few years has spoiled me. I don't want to rock the boat."

"You and I both, Em, on a lighter note, do you think Erin will ever let her guard down completely with Delores? It's been almost two years since Eric and Delores got married. Eric seems to be happy and I think they make a great family." Arlene played with an ink pen she had in her hand.

"Come on, Lennie. Are you saying you totally trust Delores? I know she's not physically dangerous, but if her own son still has mixed feelings, can you blame Erin for being cautious?"

"I learned so much from therapy, Em. I know people can change and I feel like Delores is one of those people. Are you still having misgivings too?"

"Not really. Our brother is finally happy. The fact that DJ (Eric and Delores' son) decided to work with him made him happier than I have seen him since our parents died."

"I know. I see the fire in his eyes and I'm ready to support him any way I can. It did take me about a year after they were married to feel safe, and to know that she's the right person for him. My only misgiving is her tendency to be jealous."

"Tell me about it. Any female young or old besides family that gets near Eric or their home her horns comes out." Emily and Arlene shared a good laugh then Emily's face turned serious.

"Ok, Lennie. It's time we talk about you my dear friend."

"What about me, Em?"

"How are things going with you and Cedric? You haven't said much about him lately."

"Well things were going fine until he brought up the idea of me moving in with him.

This is the first relationship I had where I felt like I've been courted and put first, but instead of accepting this joyfully, I've been waiting for the other shoe to drop."

"I'm glad you're taking things slow, Lennie. Cedric is a nice guy and I hope you guys have a long life together. You make a great couple and I've never seen you so content and at peace in your life. Is this Cedric's influence or the success of your therapy?" Emily leaned forward so she could get the juicy details.

"I think it's both, Em. Now that my therapy is over I've been thinking about something that bothers me. I get the feeling that Sam is a little put out with my relationship with his brother."

"What do you mean by put out, Lennie?"

"Well sometimes I get the feeling that he wants a more personal relationship with me."

"By personal you mean more than doctor-client?"

"Yes. Whenever Cedric and I see him, the way he looks at me is sexual."

"Oh my, Lennie. He's your former therapist and Cedric's brother. What are you going to do?"

"That's just it, Em, I don't know what to do. I want to take my relationship with Cedric to the next level, but I don't want to cause a rift between the brothers. They are so close."

"Lennie, are you saying you haven't had a physical relationship with Cedric yet?" Emily was shocked because she knew her best friend was used to being highly sexual.

No, I haven't, even though I wanted to on many occasions. I really want this to work out long term."

"Long term, Lennie are you talking about marriage?" The big smile on Arlene's face answered Emily's question.

"Yes, Em, I want to spend the rest of my life with Cedric."

"I can't wait to plan your wedding, Lennie. This will be the first one that is planned and I want to make it one you won't forget. Have you guys set a date?"

Arlene laughed. "Girl, he hasn't even asked me about marriage. He just keeps hinting at the subject, but I would love to have a Thanksgiving wedding."

"Lord, I have to go, Lennie. I have a lot of planning to do on the down low. I can't wait until its official so I can get Erin and Erica to help. I guess I'll have to include Delores too." Emily stood and clapped her hands.

"Slow down Em." Arlene shook her head. She knew she wouldn't be able to contain Emily. They hugged each other and Arlene laughed as she watched Emily walk swiftly out the door.

Chapter Three

Erica knew Calvin was still wary about the firm taking on Benjamin as a client, but Benjamin did his best to convince the trio that Nina wasn't dangerous. Benjamin hired the firm to obtain the evidence he needed to prove Nina was unfit to raise their children. Calvin questioned Benjamin thoroughly until he was satisfied the women would be safe working the case. Once Calvin left, Erica and JJ continued to talk to Benjamin to get the information needed to start the case. Erica saw the relief in JJ's face when she and Calvin agreed to take the case.

Benjamin seemed genuinely concerned about the welfare of his children and soon to be ex-wife. He admitted to not spending that much time with the children in the past, but over the last six months he'd adjusted his schedule so he could be more hands on with their needs. Nina, he confided had started making trouble because she knew this would look better for Benjamin in court.

Erica and JJ had to point out to Benjamin that what Nina was doing was harassment, but he continued to brush her actions off as part of her personality. JJ explained to him that legally harassment was unwanted and unsolicited conduct on the grounds of race, gender, or sexual orientation, which had the purpose or effect of either violating the claimant's dignity, or creating an intimidating, hostile, degrading, humiliating or offensive environment for an individual. Nina's behavior fit several of those categories.

Erica took the time to further explain to Benjamin that Nina's verbal threats, derisory remarks, public humiliation, and persistent unjustified criticism were bully tactics. According to Benjamin, Nina was behaving in this manner with the children and they were starting to normalize their mother's behavior.

"Benjamin, how far do you think Nina will go to make sure you don't get custody of the children?" Erica's suspicions were on high alert.

"What exactly are you asking me, Erica? Nina is volatile, but she wouldn't do anything to harm the children. True, she hasn't been the best mom of late, but I don't doubt her love for our children."

"Benjamin, it seems you feel she wouldn't harm them physically, but everything she's done to try to turn the children against you is mental and emotional abuse." Unlike JJ, Erica didn't have a friendship with

Benjamin to protect, and she would be the one handling most of the case work. It was imperative he understand.

"Ben, I see where Erica is going with this train of thought." JJ interjected. "We have to be able to anticipate any move Nina makes and that's hard if we don't have a firm grip on her mental status."

"JJ, to be honest with you ladies, it's hard to say what Nina may do next. She is nowhere near the sweet girl I fell in love with years ago. I know she's been cheating on me. She never tried to hide that, but now her drinking is getting out of control. I've come home a few times to find her passed out with no one keeping an eye on the children. I think she is doing more than drinking, but I don't have any proof of that right now."

"That's where we come in Ben. I think we have enough information to get started. We'll be in touch soon." Erica said.

Nina was sitting in her dad's home office trying to convince him to help her with her divorce and custody case. She was livid that he believed the children were better off with Benjamin and refused to lift a finger to help her. She understood she had made mistakes, but a parent was supposed to be there to love and support their children in their time of need. Her dad was retired from the FBI and had many connections he could use to ensure she not only got custody of her children but also a nice settlement from Benjamin. Sitting across the desk from him, Nina was fearful that she had burned her last bridge with talking him into helping her.

"Daddy, please, you can't seriously take Ben's side on this. I'm your daughter."

"You're my daughter when it's convenient for you. When was the last time you called or came to see me and didn't have your hand out or need something?"

"Daddy, please. Why are you behaving like this? I need you on my side. Ben had the nerve to hire a private investigator and he told Pastor Collins that our therapy sessions were a waste of time."

"What the hell do you expect? You've taken the man through the ringer over the last few years. I told you he was going to get fed up with your immature behavior."

"Well, if you won't help for me think about the children. Until very recently, Ben hasn't had time for them and don't get me started on his not attending any of their activities."

"How else is he supposed to support his family if he doesn't work? If his wife got off her butt and put her degree to use maybe he wouldn't be away from home as much." Nathan was sick and tired of the mess his daughter created in her life.

"My place is at home with my children, Daddy."

"Little girl, don't try to pull that bull with me because I know better. The children are in school and activities until early evening."

"Well it's not like I'm not trying to find work. You know it's hard to find work in my field."

"That's a copout, Nina. I've pulled strings for you in the past and each time you've found one excuse after another why the position

28

wouldn't work out. You prefer to have your time free so you can booze and cheat on a man that was once deeply in love with you."

"Ever since I started dating, Ben you've always sided with that fool. Why do you always have to take his side? I know you wanted a son and ended up with me."

"This discussion is over, Nina. I can't in good faith support you with my grandchildren's health and well-being at stake. I know Benny told you that if you cleaned up your act you guys could discuss joint custody later."

"Why do you and he think that he's going to get custody of my children?"

"Because your life is a mess, and you don't have means to provide a stable home."

"There is a thing called alimony and child support. I'm not walking away empty handed from this marriage."

"Nina, I love you. Please let me get you professional help."

"The only help I need is for you to help me to keep my children. I'm your only child. I may be a disappointment to you, but that doesn't mean I should lose custody of my children." Nina sobbed.

Nathan shook his head "Nina you're always trying to guilt me into doing what you want. I tell you what. Let's do this. I'll talk to Benny and the three of us can get together this week to see if we could come up with a plan that would be beneficial for all concerned. Make no mistake; I'll still be for the children to stay in the home with their dad. You can come back here if you like or I can assist you with getting your own place."

"Is that the best you can come up with, Dad?"

"Yes dear, I'm afraid that's the best solution for all involved."

"Well thanks for nothing, Dad." Nina stood and left her dad's office slamming the door.

Chapter Four

Benjamin's parents arrived on Thursday to take the children to Florida where they would attend an exclusive camp for the summer. Nina had blown a gasket, pronouncing it poor parenting to have the children miss their last week of school. She was even more upset her dad agreed it was better for them to go to camp. Benjamin hoped things would settle down by the time the children came back home at the end of August. Nathan had agreed to mediate a conversation with Benjamin and Nina once they were alone.

"Okay, let's get down to business." Nathan said. "I know things have been bad for you guys for a long time now, but for the children's sake, you guys must get this situation under control before they return."

"Dad, I know you're not going to try to play marriage counselor with us. You've made it crystal clear you're on that fool's side."

"There is no need to call me names, Nina." Benjamin said irritated.

"Nina, cut that out. We're here to address these issues in an adult manner." Nathan interjected.

"Sure Dad, whatever you say."

"Stop being sarcastic little girl."

"How should I feel? My own dad thinks I'm a horrible mom and wife that don't deserve custody of her children." Nina rolled her eyes at her dad.

"Nina, we discussed this at length the other day. What we need to do now is come to terms with the marriage being over and see how the two of you can work together to co-parent my grandchildren."

"How can you say co-parent when you support him taking full custody of my children?"

"That's only for the time being. You will be able to have joint custody once you get your life back in order. Take this time to work on you. I can help you look for employment so you won't have so much time on your hands after you've gotten help with your issues."

"Dad, you do realize I'm thirty-eight not eight. I get enough of him trying to run my life and tell me what I need to be doing." Nina pointed towards Benjamin.

"Nina, I know things are over between us as a married couple, but I would like to remain friends so we can be sure the children's needs are met."

"Oh, look at Mr. Nice throwing out crumbs to the misfit."

"I'm not going to put up with your tantrums, Nina. Let's keep this civil and come up with a plan so this won't get ugly." Benjamin said calmly.

"It won't get ugly if I get to keep this house with all the contents," Nina used her fingers to count off the things she wanted. "My car and the SUV, alimony, and child support."

"That's not going to happen. The only support I will give you is to make sure you enter a facility to get help. After you're released and stable we can discuss joint custody. I will also help you get on your feet, but you must look for work to support yourself. The children and I will stay here. I will not uproot them from the only home they've ever known."

"That's not going to work, BJ wants to stay with me and as far as Brianna is concerned she'll be okay once we're on our own." Nina said smugly.

"This isn't getting us anywhere, Nina and it doesn't make any sense to keep going around in circles. Will you be ready to get your life together and get help for your problems?" Nathan scolded.

"Daddy, the only problem I have is that you guys won't leave me alone. I'm not an addict and I'm a good mom."

"Correction, you were a good mom. I'm tired of walking on eggshells around your issues, Nina. Now all you want to do is get high and spread hateful verbal abuse to anyone that walks onto your path." Benjamin said.

"You go straight to hell, Ben. You can't prove I've been high a day in my life and just because you have my dad on your side doesn't mean you're guaranteed to get my children. I'll see you in court." Nina grabbed her purse and stormed out the door.

"I'm sorry, Nathan. I truly want to co-parent with Nina, but as you can see, she is out of control. I hope she doesn't end up hurting herself."

"Well, I've been considering treatment centers that will help her, but if she won't go in voluntarily, it's not going to work. There's an in-patient facility in Battle Creek that I think will be the perfect place for

Nina to get the help she needs. They have a specialized program for women."

"I'll do whatever I can to help you, Nathan. Nina is the mother of my children. I do care about her well-being.

"I'll get the information to you. But for the time being, I hope you guys can hash out your problems while the children are away."

"I'll do my best. I plan on taking a few weeks off work to get my affairs in order."

"Son, I'm sorry this didn't work out for you and my daughter, but please know if you or the children need anything, all you have to do is ask." Nathan shook Benjamin's hand and left the house with a sad look on his face.

It had been a long week for Arlene. Cedric said he wanted to spend the entire weekend with her with no distractions. Arlene didn't know what to read into this, but hoped it was because he wanted to talk about their future together. She also wanted to talk to Cedric about his brother. It was strange to call Dr. Baker by his first name. As her therapist, Arlene had been completely   A   comfortable with him, but lately it seemed his attitude had changed. He had encouraged her to move on with her life and consider dating again, until Samuel found out she was dating his brother. Then, all his earlier encouragement went out the window. Arlene appreciated how much Samuel helped her deal with issues from her past, especially the fear she felt after the hit-and-run.

On occasion, when she and Cedric ran into Samuel, Arlene felt uncomfortable in his presence. And there were even times he stopped by her office unannounced for no apparent reason saying he was in the neighborhood. She had mentioned this to Cedric, but he blew it off as her being paranoid. Arlene confided in Emily that she felt Sam had tried to flirt with her when they were alone. Arlene may have been out of the dating scene for a while, but she knew when someone was trying to take it to the next level and she didn't want her concerns about Cedric's brother to come between her and Cedric.

Emily told Arlene to follow her instincts and if she didn't feel right with Samuel's impromptu visits she should ask him not to stop by unannounced. Before leaving the office for the weekend, Arlene called Emily to let her know about her plans for the next few days.

"Em, it's time to get your head out of those papers and head home to your husband. Randy is going to think you're avoiding him." Randy was also the police chief.

"Well, looks like I'm not the only one still at work, Lennie."

"I'm all shut down for the weekend. I just wanted to touch base with you before I went home."

"You know I'm going to be impatiently waiting to hear about your interruptions free weekend."

"Ha! That makes two of us. I'm hoping he proposes. Then on the other hand I'm terrified because this will be number five."

"Just look at it this way, the other four times you've been married were practice runs for the real thing."

"I love you, Em. You always have something positive to say about everything."

"That's because you're a very special person who deserves a very special man to love you."

"I never thought I would get over David Jr. I know I was way too old for him, Em, but he brought a spark back into my life.

"David Jr. was put into your life for a reason, Lennie, just as he was taken out for a reason. You're very happy with Cedric, and David Jr. is a happily married man with twin sons and a thriving business so everything worked out the way it was supposed to work out. I think it is nice how he reaches out to me every so often to find out how you're doing."

"I'm happy he's found a new lease on life. I'm also glad he is keeping tight reins on his nutty dad."

"That's not fair, Lennie. David worked hard to overcome his issues just like you and I."

"Em, we were having issues because of what others did to us. David was a fruit cake all on his own." An angry look appeared on Arlene's face just thinking about those involved in her hit-and-run.

"It's time to change the subject. Make sure you call me as soon as you accept the proposal this weekend."

"Aren't you putting the cart before the horse, my dear friend?"

"No, we're just waiting on confirmation. I already have the women ready to proceed as soon as it's all official."

"Okay, Mrs. Positive, I'll be sure to update you. Have a great weekend, Em."

"You too, Lennie, make sure you behave yourself."

"You know I will. I'm reformed remember." Arlene let out a naughty laugh before she ended their call.

Chapter Five

Erica and JJ sat in the conference room going over Benjamin's case. They were expecting him within the hour. Since both he and Nina agreed divorce was a foregone conclusion, their primary focus was child custody. Benjamin had been spending more time with the children over the last six months. Keeping the family home would also work in his favor. As a condition of his grandfather's will, he couldn't add anyone's name to the deed and ownership of the home had to remain within the family.

The knock on the conference room door brought both women to their feet.

"Good morning, ladies." Benjamin said.

"Good morning, Ben." Erica and JJ said in unison.

"What do you ladies have for me today?" He asked.

"We've been working on the angle for custody since this will be the most critical issue." Erica informed him.

"And we still have surveillance on Nina." JJ chimed in.

"That's good to hear. I've sent the children to a camp in Florida for the summer. I have a feeling Nina will fight tooth and nail and things could get very ugly. I didn't want the children to have a front row seat to the madness." Ben told the ladies.

"I think that was a great idea Ben, but I bet Nina didn't feel the same." JJ smirked.

"That's an understatement. We had a brief meeting with her dad after my parents and the children left, and she lit into both of us. She basically called her dad a traitor for siding with me on the custody issue."

"Speaking of custody, let's go over a few things." Erica pointed out to Benjamin that the judge looked at many factors upon considering the best interest of the child/children: the children's age, the parents' living situation, the parents' willingness to co-parent, child preference, and the continuity/stability of the children's environment. In considering the age factor the judge usually looks at who has been the primary caregiver for most of the children's lives. Though this factor was a strike against Benjamin, the parental living situation looked good for him because the house was his. This would also allow the children to be close to school

41

and their extracurricular activities. As for willingness to co-parent, Erica suggested they bring to the judge's attention that Nina has been working hard to turn the children against Benjamin. The child preference wasn't a factor since most courts take this into consideration with children twelve or older. Erica also informed Benjamin a custody evaluator might be assigned. Lastly, Erica explained when the judge looked at the continuity and stability of the children he or she would want to change the children's lives as least as possible.

"This is a lot to think about." Benjamin said rubbing his hand across his face. "I really don't want to tear Nina apart because that will hurt the children. They love their mom, and I still care enough about her to want her to get the help she desperately needs."

"Ben, I know this is a touchy situation, but it may come to a point where you're going to have to pull out all the stops to get custody of your children." JJ touched his arm. "I know that might be difficult to hear, but we need to prepare you for the possibility of a big fight. You know Nina is determined to keep your children, the house, and other martial assets."

"I know." Benjamin nodded his head. "Is there anything else you ladies have for me before we end this meeting? I think I need some time alone to process all this."

"Yes, there is. The court will also look at the parent who has the best plan for the children. My brother is putting together a document that will fully outline the plan you have for your children. He will make the court aware of your willingness to co-parent with Nina once she gets professional help. Visitation and possible joint-custody will also be addressed. All of this will ensure the children's stability by keeping them in the home in which they were raised, while continuing their activities, and most importantly, providing a positive environment." Erica wanted Benjamin to have this report as a supplement to what his divorce attorney put together.

"Okay, anything else?"

"Nope, I think that's it, Ben. We'll be in touch soon." Erica shook Ben's hand. "Make sure you continue to try to work things out with Nina regarding the children. We have our work cut out for us, but I feel very strongly that we could win this case." After giving JJ a brief hug and shaking Erica's hand, the ladies walked Benjamin to the door and went back to work.

Arlene sat in her office reliving the best weekend she had in her life. Cedric had dinner waiting when she arrived home and surprised her by having Eric show up right after dinner to have a drink with them. Eric seemed equally surprised as to why he was called over to meet with them. Cedric got straight to the point telling Eric how much he loved Arlene and how much he looked forward to being part of their family. He then asked Eric if he could have Arlene's hand in marriage. This old-fashioned gesture made both Eric and Arlene laugh, which seemed to hurt Cedric's feelings. After clearing up the awkward moment, Eric turned to ask Arlene how she felt about the proposal. One look at the glowing expression on his sister's face was answer enough for Eric, and he gave Cedric his blessing.

Arlene was so tired that night, but calling Emily to tell her she was going to be the next Mrs. Cedric Dwayne Baker was the highlight of

Arlene's night. On Saturday, she and Cedric announced the news to Samuel. Samuel's reaction to their announcement disturbed Arlene. He didn't seem as happy as Eric and the rest of the family. She knew when someone in despair was putting on a good face because she had been guilty of that most of her life. Sam was Cedric's only living relative and she wanted to be accepted. Thinking of their recent conversation, Arlene wasn't sure if that would happen.

"Arlene, are you sure this is a wise decision?" Samuel had a stern look on his face.

"Why would you ask me such a question? Of course I'm sure. Your brother is the best thing that's happened in my life in a long time."

"Sammy, what are you doing man?" Cedric asked.

"Big brother, I'm not trying to rain on your parade, but it's hard sometimes to separate personal from professional. I know firsthand what Arlene has been through and I'm trying to make sure she doesn't relapse."

"You act like I was on drugs or something, Sam. I came to see you when I was at a down point in my life because some fools from the past decided to take revenge against me for things they made happen."

"Arlene, we both know your issues went farther than a few years back. You've been struggling with many issues since childhood."

"Issues I addressed and overcame. I don't want to talk about this again, Sam."

The finality in Arlene's voice didn't leave room for further discussion. Cedric had asked Samuel to leave and the two of them enjoyed the rest of the weekend. On Sunday, she received so many calls about her engagement; Arlene knew Emily had made her rounds. Erica's call was the most sentimental because she told Arlene she was more like a second mom than an aunt and she was happy Arlene had finally found true love.

Arlene called for her assistant. It was time for her to get back to work. She was meeting with Emily later in the day for lunch, and she wanted to enjoy her lunch break without work hanging over her head.

Chapter Six

A week had passed since Benjamin sent the children away to camp, and Nina finally realized she was fighting a losing battle and going about getting what she wanted the wrong way. She knew she wasn't going to get the house in the divorce settlement because of that stupid clause in Benjamin's grandfather's will. She thought she would be able to talk Benjamin into letting her stay in the house with the children after the divorce, but she was sorely mistaken. She decided to cut her losses for now and move in with her dad. There was no way she was going to stay under the same roof with that fool, Benjamin now that the children were gone for the entire summer.

Things may work out to her advantage living with her dad. She would have more time to convince him to side with her if she was living with him, and since he had a big house there was plenty of room for her and the children to make a home. She had less than a month to prepare for the divorce hearing, and she was going to make damn sure she walked out of the courtroom with a decent settlement. Her attorney told her more than once that Benjamin's settlement offer was beyond generous and she would be wise to accept it, but there was no way she was giving up her children. Not only would that take the last little control she had over Benjamin, it would also cut into the money she depended on getting from the divorce.

The private investigator Benjamin hired was really cramping her style. She couldn't move freely and had to lay low. If they found out she was doing more than just drinking to cope with her problems, she would most definitely lose custody. She had been getting high so long she didn't know when it had gotten out of control. Nina knew she had to be careful once she moved in with her dad. Since she was packing, she decided to pack all her things so she wouldn't have to come back to this house of horrors. July 11th couldn't come soon enough. She was ready to see what the judge would say.

Nina and Benjamin had been sleeping in separate bedrooms for the last six months, which afforded Nina more privacy than when they slept together. Sometimes Nina looked at Benjamin and could see the man she fell in love with, but she didn't want to think about that because then she would have to think about how she destroyed her life. Looking back, she wished she had followed up on some of the leads her dad had given her regarding employment. She needed her free time and wanted to be able to tell the court she was a stay at home mom to strengthen her chances of custody.

Nina had just finished packing her toiletries when the doorbell rang. She went downstairs and answered it disappointed to see her soon to be ex-sister-in-law, Evelyn on the other side.

"What do you want, Lyn?"

"Hello to you too, Nina. Why do you always have to be so rude?"

"That's one thing I won't miss, having to put up with your spoiled behind."

"You're a drama queen, Nina. You won't be missed. I always thought my brother could do so much better than you. I'm glad he finally came to his senses."

Nina never liked Evelyn because Benjamin always catered to her every whim. "I don't have time for your bullshit little girl." Nina told her sister-in-law, leaving her in the living room while she went upstairs to double check her packing. She called her dad to let him know she was ready. Nina took one final look around the spare bedroom she'd been using and sat on the chair that was in the corner, waiting for her dad to arrive.

Benjamin had just finished a short meeting with the executive team at the bank. His sister walked into his office, and he could tell by the look on her face that she wasn't happy about something. He hoped she wasn't there to ask about the lead teller opening she'd been trying to talk him into giving her. There were at least three or four more qualified candidates for the position, so he would have to tell her what he'd been telling her for the last few weeks. NO. Lyn flopped down in one of the chairs in front of his desk and didn't waste any time getting to the point.

"I just came from your house and that hag was there."

"Lyn, there's no reason for name calling."

"I beg to differ. I stayed around until her dad picked her up to make sure she didn't take anything that didn't belong to her."

"Why do I get the feeling you are enjoying this a little too much?"

"Because I am, it's about time she moved out. I can tell from the sneaky look in her eyes she has something devious planned."

"Baby girl you are much too young to be so distrustful."

"I know you're not sitting there saying you trust that woman."

"I'm not. And I don't, but I have my reasons. Nina has gone out of her way to steer clear of you."

"That's only because she knows I will call her out on her mess."

"Well, we have less than a month before all of this is settled."

"Benny, promise me you'll be careful. She left the house too easily. At first she refused to leave and now all of the sudden she couldn't get out of there fast enough."

"It's because the children are gone for the summer. She can't use them to get back at me. Her dad found a good facility he hopes he'll be able to talk her into signing herself into."

"You know that's not going to happen. She still swears up and down that she doesn't have a problem."

"Well, we all know she does so either she gets help or I'm going to have to file for sole custody of the children with her only seeing them in a supervised environment."

"That's not going to scare that hag. She's plotting something. I hope the firm you hired is as good as you say, so when you go to court you'll have all your ducks in a row."

"They are. As a matter of fact, I have an appointment with them Friday morning for an update. The focus will be on custody since my attorney feels he can get Nina to accept the settlement offer."

"Why are you giving her anything? You're going to have the children. She is the one that needs to get off her behind and work and pay child support."

"'Come on, baby girl. She deserves a settlement after the length of time we've been married."

"That is my cue to leave. She's been living high off your money for years. She isn't handicapped. She could have gotten a job. You had a housekeeper and at one point a nanny to care for the children."

"I've made my mistakes, baby girl. I was away from home most of the time building my career, and I missed out on a lot of the children's growing years. That's going to hurt me in court. I know it wasn't right for Nina to try to turn them against me, but she was fighting for what she thought was rightfully hers."

"She still is, so don't get it twisted thinking she's going to roll over and play dead just because she moved out of your house."

"You don't have to worry about that, little sister. I know Nina will fight dirty. I don't expect her to give up on her attempt to get the children."

"If you know all of this then why does it seem like you're going easy on her? She's going to pull out all the stops. I know she got it in her crazy mind now that she'll be able to provide a stable home for the children living in that big house with her dad.

"It doesn't matter what she thinks. The judge will not uproot the children if it's not totally necessary. I have to work on my relationship with BJ. Nina has put it into his head that I don't care about them. That's why I plan on going to visit them at camp."

53

"Before I leave, big brother, will it be okay if I move in for the summer so I can save for my own apartment? I can't take it any longer where I'm at."

"Sure. I told you a while back you could move back home."

"I know, but I didn't want a front row seat seeing the way that hag degrades you and constantly tries to turn the children against you."

"Well, she's going to find out the hard way in court that that was a big mistake. I know the children aren't old enough to have a say in where they stay, but if they are questioned they will tell about the negative things their mom has been doing."

"Poor babies, at ten and six, they shouldn't have to go through that drama. I pray they won't have to take sides."

"It's been a long day, baby girl. I'm tired. I'm going to head home. You can move back any time you want. You can use the room next to Brianna's if you don't want to move back into your old room. Nina's been using that one."

"I know. After she left, I went up there to check on things. I must say I'm surprised it was clean. I expected her to do some damage to the house before she left."

"She knows she has to be on her best behavior if she stands a chance of getting the children. When are you moving in?"

"Today, I'm going to pack a few things for the rest of the week and move the rest of my things over the weekend."

Benjamin walked Evelyn to the door and headed out behind her for some much-needed rest.

Chapter Seven

Erica and JJ had paperwork spread all over the conference room table. Their assistant had already brought their morning coffee. They were studying some of the surveillance photos their team had gathered when there was a knock on the door. Both ladies said come in at the same time. Their assistant peeped her head in and said they had a visitor. Before the assistant could announce her, Nina pushed her way into the conference room.

"Good morning ladies. I'm Nina Nicholson-Bailey. But you already know who I am, JJ."

Erica gathered the paperwork spread across the table stuffed it in the folders, and offered Nina a seat towards the end of the table away from their classified materials. Nina declined.

"Good morning, Mrs. Bailey, I'm Erica Blackstone. As you mentioned, you already know JJ." Erica approached and offered her a handshake.

Nina folded her arms, refusing to shake Erica's hand. "Yes, I'm well aware of JJ. She's a close friend to my soon to be ex-husband...too close."

Erica and JJ exchanged a glance.

"Nina, how have you been?" JJ asked, choosing to ignore Nina's snide remark.

"I would be better if you didn't insist on butting into my personal life, JJ."

"Why are you here, Nina? How can we help you?"

"I know Ben hired your company to keep tabs on me. You can help me by dropping the case, because it's not a good idea.

"This topic isn't up for discussion, Nina." JJ said.

"Not what I want to hear, JJ."

"Mrs. Bailey, we're very busy. Would you mind leaving?" Erica didn't want the confrontation between JJ and Nina to spiral out of control.

"Not until you guys back off. My life is none of your business, and no matter what you come up with I'm not giving up my children."

"Like Erica said, Nina, it's time for you to leave." JJ insisted.

Nina stormed out in a huff. Then stopped and turned to Erica and JJ.

"Listen to what I have to say. Back off and leave me the hell alone." She slammed the door and left.

"Wow, she makes me a little anxious. She's pretty high strung." Erica said.

"More like loony to be exact. I forgot how unbalanced she could be at times."

"I don't know, JJ. We need to have a serious talk about this situation when Ben arrives."

"I know we do, but don't let her keep us from the work we should be doing on this case."

"Let's get back to work then, so we can be ready for Ben."

Erica and JJ sat back down at the table and returned to work.

Arlene placed an urgent call to Emily, Eric, and Erin to meet her at her condo. They had taken the afternoon off from work and now sat around in her den enjoying refreshments and making small talk.

"Okay, sister. We're all here. We've eaten. We've chatted. You know I'm not one for small talk. What was so urgent we needed to meet right away?" Erin asked.

Arlene gave a nervous chuckled.

"Thank you all for coming over so quickly." She wrung her hands together. "Cedric and I have set a date for our wedding, Saturday, November twenty-six." Arlene gently touched Emily's hand.

"That's wonderful, Lennie, but it doesn't give us much time to plan." Emily said.

"But that's not the reason I called you guys over today. Cedric was excited to share the date we'd chosen with Sam and it didn't go well at all." Arlene was guarded with her words.

"Lennie, what are you not telling us?" Emily asked.

"I've already told you guys we weren't getting full support from Sam, but when we told him the wedding date, Sam went on a tirade."

"I don't like where this is headed, Arlene. You're finally happy and at peace. I don't want to see that destroyed by anyone." Eric stood and paced. "Maybe it's time I had a man-to-man talk with the good doctor."

"I agree with Eric. It sounds like the good doctor needs therapy." Erin added.

"Lennie, tell us everything that happened when you guys told Samuel you set a date." Emily said.

"Well, we had just finished eating dinner and the guys were in here talking about sports,
And believe it or not, I was in the kitchen cleaning. All of a sudden, their voices grew louder. I came in here, and they were face to face looking like they were ready to come to blows."

"Oh my God Lennie, what happened to change the mood so drastically?" Emily asked.

"It seemed Sam had a problem with Cedric telling him about our setting the wedding date. Sam said I was rushing into something I wasn't ready for and was headed for a relapse." Arlene responded.

"That's it." Eric's voice boomed with anger. "I've heard enough. I'll be getting with

Samuel today and I will tell him in no uncertain terms to stay the hell out of your personal life. He's supposed to be able to keep his professional life separate from his private life."

"Eric, calm down. I'm sure we can come up with a plan to alleviate the situation." Emily walked over to her big brother and offered him a comforting hug.

"No, Emily. I made the mistake years ago not confronting a situation head on. I have no intention of making that mistake again." Eric thought about Emily's breakup with David.

"Eric, you know I can handle myself. I'm not saying that Em couldn't, but I've eaten people worse than Sam for lunch and dinner. I got this. Please trust me on this one, and if the situation gets out of hand, you will be the first call I make." Arlene prayed they would be able to talk Eric down.

"I think that's sensible, Eric. Arlene is the most in control person I know outside of you. If she says she can handle this situation you should give her the chance to do so. This is what she does best." Erin added.

"Ladies, I know you all mean well. But Samuel is going off the deep end, and we have enough to deal with since Rica and JJ decided to take on a potentially dangerous case. We need to make sure this issue doesn't get out of hand."

"Calvin is working with Benjamin's divorce attorney and he's assured there are no problems there. The custody is a different matter. Since Nina moved in with her dad, she is confident that she has a better chance of getting custody. After talking to Erica this morning, I'm worried about her and JJ. I'd say Nina is more confident than ever." Emily rubbed her head to ease the tension.

"I'll be meeting with Rica, Junior, and JJ later today. I don't like that situation either, but don't think you ladies will deter me from setting Samuel straight. He should have no say in what his brother does or doesn't do. And he most definitely shouldn't have a say in your life, Arlene." Eric said.

"I must admit, the way Sam has been acting worries me a little, but he's trying to do what's best for his brother. Sam knows I have a checkered past and that's what is so disconcerting to him about my relationship with Cedric. It's been a rough ten years since Cedric's wife died."

"Lennie, I'm sure it has been. But it's up to Cedric to proceed with his life as he sees fit without his meddling brother trying to come between the two of you." Emily stated.

"I totally agree with Emily. Cedric needs to step up and put his brother in his place and tell him to stay out of your relationship, Arlene." Erin said.

"I'll handle it. I promise. I just wanted to keep you guys posted on the latest. Thank you all for coming over. Em, I'll get with you and the women soon to go over the details I'm sure you've already arranged.

Arlene walked the trio to the door and went back to the den to think about how she was going to approach the subject with Cedric.

Chapter Eight

Early Monday morning Erica received a call on her way to the office from the school's headmistress. The reluctance to give Erica any details about her twin girls over the phone frustrated her. She prayed for peace and that she would make it to her destination safely, but she couldn't imagine what was so important that she had to rush to the school. The girls left home this morning fine. If one of them had been hurt at school, surely the headmistress would have told her that over the phone. She didn't want to call (her husband, Jonathan) and interrupt his big meeting until she knew what was going on. Erica arrived, parked her car and made her way into the school.

Erica entered the headmistress's office and rushed over to her girls. "Girls, are you ok?" She breathed a sigh of relief, neither looked physically hurt.

"We're okay, Mommy. We asked Headmistress Thomas not to call you, but she insisted she had to have you come down to meet with her." Erica was proud of her oldest daughter by four minutes. Shereese reminded Erica of a miniature Arlene and was the most outgoing and outspoken of all her children.

"Girls, I need the two of you to go to Mrs. Byrd's office while I speak with your mom." Headmistress Thomas's nasally voice irritated Erica.

"Mrs. Clark, I apologize for the inconvenience to your morning routine, but this matter couldn't wait." Headmistress Thomas pulled out a couple of sheets of paper and handed them to Erica. Erica looked at the papers and almost fell out of the chair she'd sat in. One was a caricature of a woman looking exactly like Erica smoking a crack pipe, and the other one was the same depiction of Erica engaged in sexual acts with several men.

"Where did these come from, Headmistress Thomas?"

"They were in a packet left by a teacher a part of the day's lesson plan. A student disseminated the handouts for the substitute teacher. The kids started talking about the pictures and quite naturally, the girls became upset. An altercation developed among them and a few other students."

"What type of altercation? Were my girls fighting?" Erica was befuddled. "Who would do something like this to small children?"

"That's not the worst of it, Mrs. Clark. It's my understanding the same pictures were sent to your younger twins' class as well."

"I can't believe something like this has happened. What have you done to get to the bottom of this situation, Headmistress Thomas?"

"We will launch a full investigation, Mrs. Clark. However, under the circumstances I thought you might want to take the children home at least for today."

"Of course I'll do that. But I need to know how something like this happened."

"I'm sorry," Headmistress Thomas shook her head. "We don't have any answers for you right now, Mrs. Clark. Your younger children will be brought to the office so you won't have to go to the other building to retrieve them. They were quite upset."

"There is no truth to the allegations in those pictures. My children shouldn't have been exposed to something so harmful."

"I understand, Mrs. Clark. We promise to get to the bottom of this. We'll inform you when the matter has been properly addressed."

"Wait a minute, Headmistress Thomas. It sounds like you expect me to keep my children out of school while you do your investigation."

"Please, Mrs. Clark. This has never happened at our school before. We need to make sure we give all our students the best educational environment possible without any unnecessary distractions.

"Excuse me. I need to check on my children." Erica left the office, picked up her children, and headed home. Still not wanting to disturb Jonathan, she called her mom and asked her to come over as soon as possible. Erica also called JJ to let her know it would be a few hours before she made it into the office due to a family emergency.

JJ had been at work for almost an hour when Erica called and told her she had a family emergency. JJ didn't mind; she needed a chance to wake up. JJ loved being a mom, but the late night feedings were getting to her. Thankfully, Lewis took some of them. If he didn't she would have been in a world of trouble. JJ sat at her desk thinking about her handsome husband. She looked up surprised to see him standing in her doorway with an angry look on his face.

"Honey, what are you doing here?" JJ asked.

"We need to talk, JJ."

"Okay, but can this wait until I get home? Erica had a family emergency this morning so I have to do some work on Ben's case."

"That's exactly what I'm here to talk to you about. Do you want to tell me what's going on with you and your newest client?"

"Lewis, I don't like your tone. Why do you sound angry?"

"Please answer my question, JJ."

"Ben has been a friend for a long time. Before he came to us about his case, I hadn't had any contact with him for months."

"Are you sure about that, JJ?"

"Lewis just spit it out. What are you asking me?"

"Have you ever had a physical relationship with Benjamin?"

"Of course not, I told you we're just friends."

"Well how do you explain these?" Lewis gave JJ the envelope he had in his hand and she stared at him while she opened them. Once she had the pictures out of the envelope, all she could do was look at them with a shocked look on her face. The pictures were clearly of her and Benjamin in some compromising positions.

"Where did you get these, Lewis?"

"They were delivered to my office a few days ago, but I just had the chance to look at them this morning. I've also been getting phone calls with someone breathing on the other end, but they never say anything."

"I don't know what to say, babe. These had to have been photo-shopped. This is some crazy shit right here and I bet you my next paycheck I know who's behind it."

"That isn't making me feel any better, JJ. I know where you are going with that train of thought, and if this Nina person would do something like this, there is no telling what else she may have up her sleeve."

"I'm not going to let that crazy heifer run my business or tell me what cases I can or can't take. I hope you don't believe these are authentic."

"I don't know what to think, JJ. They look like the real thing to me."

"Well, they're not real. You know I don't roll like that, honey. I wouldn't mess with a married man or any man for that matter. I'm totally dedicated to our family."

"I know you are, babe." Lewis walked around the desk and hugged JJ. "I'm sorry for barging in here all angry. It's just that…Well, seeing you in these pictures and then the phone calls…I just got a little paranoid."

"I love you, Lewis Wheeler, and only you. The only man I'm gonna be in a compromising position with is you." JJ kissed her husband.

They talked for a little while longer before she walked him to the door. JJ was mad as hell. She couldn't wait to tell Erica about Nina's new level of crazy. It was time to put a stop to this madness before someone got hurt.

Chapter Nine

Erica was surprised when Calvin showed up with Emily. Emily told Erica that Calvin was at her office when she called and he insisted on coming to see what was wrong. Erica had put the younger twins down for a nap, and the older twins were in their room. As soon as they were all seated in Erica's office she explained about the call from Headmistress Thomas. She was ashamed to show them the pictures, but she couldn't get out of it.

"What the heck is going on, Erica? Does the school have any idea how this happened?" Calvin was irate.

"The Headmistress said they would investigate and get back with me as soon as possible. The thing is they apparently don't want the twins to come back to school until the matter has been resolved. I haven't had the chance to tell Jonathan what's going on yet, but I left a message with his assistant for him to call me as soon as he was done with his meeting."

"Could this have anything to do with Nina's visit last week? I knew nothing good would come from you and JJ taking this case." Calvin rubbed his face in frustration.

"I don't know. Give me a few minutes to check in with JJ. Maybe she can shed some light on that crazy woman." Emily and Calvin went into the kitchen to get some snacks. They walked back in the room and Emily almost dropped the tray she carried.

"What's wrong, baby girl?" She couldn't get around the desk fast enough.

Erica brought Emily and Calvin up to speed on what transpired at the office between JJ and Lewis. There was no doubt Nina was behind all of this.

"Erica, it's not too late to drop this case. This woman is on the same level as Clarissa and Jessica.

"The damage is already done, big brother. Even if we dropped the case, Nina might not stop this foolishness. We've set up a meeting with Ben for later this afternoon to discuss the latest events."

"That's my clue to leave. I'm headed to the school to see what they are doing about this craziness. I'll call Uncle Eric to see if he can meet me there. Once we're done there, we'll meet you at your office so we can be there for your meeting with Benjamin." Calvin gave his mom and sister a kiss on their cheeks and left. The school will give him some answers or else he and Erica would pull their children out. Two of Calvin's three children also attended the twin's school.

"Mom, I'm mortified my children had to see such garbage. Who would draw pictures like that?" Shereese told the class they better not say a word about me and that those pictures were a lie." Even though she was sad, Erica smiled at her daughter's boldness. Shereese never missed a chance to speak her mind.

"Don't worry, baby girl. We're going to get to the bottom of this. If that woman is crazy enough to take on all of us she is more foolish than you all think."

"That's not all I'm worried about thought. If she would go through these lengths to get us to drop the case, what else would she do to get what she wants?"

"She's a loose cannon, baby girl. I'm starting to think it was a big mistake to take on Benjamin's case."

"Mom, we can't let fools like Nina dictate to us what cases we can and cannot take. I appreciate you coming over, but now that the nanny is back, I'm going to head to the office." Erica went to check on the younger twins who were still asleep. The older twins were in their room playing dress-up. Before she left, Shereese told her mom when they went back to school she better not hear any talking or whispering about those stupid pictures or she was going to put them in their place. Telling her outspoken daughter to watch her mouth, Erica kissed them on their cheeks and headed out the door with her mom. She gave her mom a big hug and said thank you for rushing over. Erica smiled all the way to the office thinking about the colorful choice of words that came out of Shereese's mouth.

Nina sat in her dad's office getting high. It was time to strike while the iron was hot. The trump card she had in place was going to blow the mind of both of those arrogant heifers. They thought she would roll over and play dead. Well, she would show them. She knew they were thinking the feeble things that happened so far were bad. Nina couldn't wait to put the main event into action. This was going to blow their minds and let them know the next time they try to take someone's children from them they would have to pay dearly.

Nina's dad was out of town for the next few weeks giving her free reign of the house. She wouldn't have to sneak around to live her life the way she wanted. Telling the housekeeper she didn't have to come back until her dad returned wasn't as easy as Nina thought it would be. Nina had to offer the old wench double time for her to take a two-week vacation. The extra pay sealed the deal. *So much for Daddy having someone here to keep an eye on me.* Nina didn't mind paying her since she used money out of the joint account Benjamin hadn't yet closed. She laughed, that fool Benjamin was paying for all her pleasures.

Nina couldn't believe he had the nerve to cancel her credit cards and close all their joint accounts. Benjamin was going to be shocked that she drained the account and there wasn't a damn thing he could do about it.

Her dad had refused to give her any money. He told her she was going to have to find a job after she received professional help and that he wasn't going to enable her any longer. Both of them could go to hell, because she wasn't going to need any of their money after she put the last phase of her plan in motion Nina's thoughts were interrupted by the sound of her phone ringing. She had been waiting all morning for this call. Smiling, Nina jumped up from her dad's office chair and hurried to get dressed.

Calvin and Eric sat in JBI's conference room discussing what happened at the school. They were livid that the school didn't have any answers to the morning incident. Headmistress Thomas was embarrassed and explained that nothing like that had ever happened at the school since its inception. She assured them the administration was working diligently on a solution. Eric asked if she told Erica to keep the children out of school until the investigation was over, and she stuttered saying it was merely a suggestion. Calvin told her the twins would be back in school tomorrow and if the school didn't want a lawsuit on their hands, they'd better have some answers sooner rather than later. What happened to both

Erica and JJ was amateurish. It was hard to believe someone as devious as Nina thought she would get away with it. Calvin wondered if it was just a smoke screen for something bigger to come. Benjamin entered the conference room interrupting their conversation. After shaking hands, the men sat at the table.

"Benjamin, did JJ tell you why she called this meeting?" Calvin asked.

"Not exactly, I figured they were able to make headway with the case."

Calvin nodded. He didn't want to step out of line. "I see. Then, let's wait for the ladies before we get started."

"While we're waiting on the ladies, can you tell us about the soon to be ex-Mrs. Bailey?" Eric inquired.

Benjamin nodded. "We met and fell in love many years ago. Nina was a sweet and kind-hearted person. Over the years, as our children grew older, she had too much idle time on her hands. Instead of going back to work or doing something constructive she turned to drinking and quite possibly drugs. She's been out of control for a few years now. I saw how it was affecting our children and decided to end the marriage and file for sole custody."

"Is this the reason she's coming apart at the seams?" Calvin asked.

"Partially, but I've also limited her access to our funds. Her dad isn't enabling her any longer neither. I think the change has been hard for her to handle."

"Ben, when the ladies get in here you'll see Nina has no intention of fighting fair or going away. I'll be honest with you like I was at the beginning, I'm more worried now than when they first took your case. I know that in their line of business they are going to run across some cases that may be dangerous, but since you are a personal friend of JJ's it could cloud her better judgment."

"I truly hope that's not the case, Calvin. I've known JJ for a long time and she's a tough cookie. I wouldn't want to put her or your sister in harm's way. If they want to drop my case, I'll have to accept that with no hard feelings."

Satisfied with Benjamin's response, Calvin nodded. The guys made small talk while they waited for Erica and JJ.

Chapter Ten

JJ couldn't believe she and Erica were still in the meeting with Benjamin, Eric, and Calvin. They had been going at it for almost two hours with no end in sight. It was after four o'clock and JJ wanted to get home to her son and husband. Thank God it was Lewis's turn to pick up Leo from daycare. JJ could see from the look on Erica's face she was ready to bring this meeting to a close. Both ladies refused to drop the case because they felt it wouldn't do any good and they weren't going to let Nina's crazy behind dictate what cases they took. Benjamin promised to have a serious talk with both Nina and her dad about getting her committed to the facility in Battle Creek. As they were wrapping up the meeting, their assistant interrupted and told JJ that Lewis was on the phone. JJ excused herself and followed the assistant to her desk.

"Hi, honey, I'm almost done here. I'll be home shortly." JJ said.

"Babe, why would you take Leo to the office instead of bringing him home?" JJ frowned. She could tell Lewis was irritated.

"What are you talking about Lewis? I don't have the baby here."

"I just left the daycare and they said you picked Leo up about an hour ago."

"I haven't been out of the office since I arrived this morning. I'm about to leave here right now. Meet me at the daycare please." JJ ended the call and told the others about her conversation with Lewis. She was too upset to drive so Eric offered to drive them all over since he had the largest vehicle. Erica told Ben they had to finish their meeting later. The four of them arrived at the daycare just as Lewis pulled up.

JJ was terrified. She entered the daycare, and the receptionist greeted her with a big smile and asked if she had forgotten something.

"What the hell are you talking about, Gwen? I haven't been here since I dropped Leo off this morning." JJ was fighting mad.

"There must be some mistake. You came in a little over an hour ago. I was surprised you picked Leo up because you said Mr. Wheeler would be picking him up today."

Hearing the commotion, the daycare manager came out to see what was happening.

"Hi, Mr. and Mrs. Wheeler, is there a problem?"

81

"You damn right there's a problem. My husband came to pick our son up and Gwen said he was picked up by me over an hour ago."

"That's correct. You picked up Leo about an hour ago."

"Listen, I'm going to say this one more time. I didn't pick my son up so where the hell is he?"

"Listen to me carefully." Erica spoke calmly. "Mrs. Wheeler and I have been in meetings all day, she didn't pick Leo up. We need to see your security footage right now so we can see what's going on here."

The manager escorted all of them to her office while she went to the utility room to get the footage. She returned and put the tape into the system set up in her office. They all were shocked when someone, the spitting image of JJ, signed Leo out and walked away with him. The manager called Gwen and told her to bring the sign-in sheet. JJ looked at the signature. The handwriting style was similar, but it wasn't hers. JJ signed her name Jasmine Wheeler when she picked up Leo, and this signature read Mrs. J. Wheeler

"I'm so sorry about all of this, Mr. and Mrs. Wheeler. Nothing like this has ever happened to us before. Gwen, call the police right away."

JJ sobbed, and Lewis tried to console her. While they waited on the police, Erica called Randy and filled him in on what was going on. He promised to come over right away. Once Randy and two uniformed officers arrived, they took the tape evidence and went over everything that happened. Erica called Benjamin and asked him to meet them at the daycare. When Benjamin arrived, they all went into the daycare's large conference room.

"You need to call Nina right now and get her crazy behind over here." JJ screamed.

"Whoa, JJ, what's the matter?" Benjamin asked.

"My son has been kidnapped." JJ started sobbing again.

"What does that have to do with Nina?" Benjamin looked around. His eyes rested on the police.

Randy took over. "Mr. Bailey, do you know where your wife is?"

"Far as I know, she's at her dad's house." Benjamin gave Randy, Nathan's address and Nina's cell phone number. He didn't know what to say to JJ and Erica. He didn't want to defend Nina, but he didn't think she would go this far. Kidnapping was a felony offense.

"Randy, I need a copy of that tape. JJ, I know this is very hard, but I'll put our resources on the case. Lewis, maybe you should take her home in case someone calls your land-line." Erica said.

"I'll send the two uniformed officers with you to get you guys set up. We're going to find your baby, JJ." With the daycare manager, Lewis, JJ, and the officers' gone Randy took Benjamin into another room to question him. Erica, Eric, and Calvin stayed in the conference room.

"This was exactly what I was afraid of Erica. I had a feeling this wasn't going to turn out well." Calvin scolded.

"JJ was insistent we could handle this case. I know all the fingers are pointing to Nina, but what if she had nothing to do with the kidnapping?" Erica was trying to make sense of who else might want to take Leo besides Nina.

"Look at everything that has happened since that woman's visit last week" Calvin said.

"We can't waste any time. Let's go get Randy and Ben so we can pay Nina a visit." Erica left the conference room with Eric and Calvin following behind. They gathered Randy and Benjamin and headed over to Nathan's house.

Randy was glad he drove the police truck instead of the cruiser to the daycare. Everyone was quiet for the first few minutes of the half hour drive to Nathan's. Benjamin prayed Nina wasn't involved in this incident. If she was, she was looking at prison time, and she wouldn't get the help she needed in prison. He tried contacting Nathan but couldn't reach him so he left a message and asked him to call as soon as possible. Half-way there, Eric expressed his disappointment in how the case was going.

"Uncle Eric, I know how you're feeling, but we need to focus on getting Leo back. Nina's actions aren't Ben's fault." Erica said.

"Eric, JJ and I go way back. I would never do anything to put her or your niece in danger. I told JJ it might be best if I hired another firm, but she said they could handle the case.

Nina has never done anything this reckless before that I'm aware of. I'm as dumbfounded as the rest of you." Benjamin said.

"When we get there, I have to do the questioning. If you guys won't be able to keep your cool, you should stay in the car." Randy knew firsthand how this family reacted when one of their own was threatened.

"That's depends on how Nina reacts to your questioning. It's bad enough if she is responsible for the other things that have been happening, but if she's responsible for Leo's kidnapping, she's bitten off more than she'll be able to chew." Erica said.

The police truck pulled into the driveway. Everyone had exited the vehicle and was headed to the front door when Benjamin suggested he call Nina first. Randy told him that wasn't a good idea. They knocked several times before Nina opened the door.

"What do you all want? Banging on my door like crazy fools." Nina looked like she had just gotten out of bed even though it was late afternoon.

"Good afternoon, I'm Chief Randy Williamson. Are you Nina Bailey?" Randy tried to be polite.

"Yes, why do you want to know?" Nina asked, giving everyone a whiff of the alcohol on her breath.

"May we come in? There are a few questions I need to ask you." Randy asked.

Without answering him, Nina moved aside to let them in but not before rolling her eyes at Erica and Benjamin. They went into the living room and waited for Nina to join them.

"Mrs. Bailey, I want to ask you a few questions about your visit to Jefferson and Blackstone Investigations last week." Randy said.

"What about it?"

"What was the reason for your visit?"

"I went there to get them to drop this stupid case. This is between me and that fool." Nina pointed towards Benjamin.

"There's no need for name calling, Mrs. Bailey." Randy said.

"Please, stop calling me that. My name is Nina."

"Okay, Nina. There have been several incidents that have happened to Erica and JJ over the last week or so. Would you know

87

anything about that?" Randy wanted to be more formal when speaking about Erica and JJ but didn't want to upset Nina further.

"I don't know what you're talking about, Chief Williamson."

"Inflammatory pictures were sent to JJ's husband and to Erica's children's school."

"Like I said, I don't know what you talking about." Nina insisted.

"Where have you been since this morning?"

"I've been here minding my business trying to get some sleep until you came banging on my door."

"Cut the bull, Nina. We all know you had something to do with JJ's son, Leo's disappearance." Erica said.

Randy glared at Erica, but she didn't care. Erica was sick of the soft line of questions.

"I don't know a Leo." Nina's expression didn't change.

"Nina, please tell me you have nothing to do with that baby's disappearance." Benjamin pleaded.

"Didn't I just say I don't know what the hell you all are talking about? Now if you'll excuse me, I must get back to bed. I have a pounding headache."

"Thank you for your time, Nina." Randy motioned for everyone to get up so they could leave.

"I guess that's what happens when you try to take people children from them." Nina smirked.

Erica turned and lurched towards Nina, but Randy grabbed her to stop her from going any further. With a deadly calm, Erica said. "Nina, I swear. If you had anything to do with what's been happening, you're going to get a one-way ticket straight to hell."

Nina let out a wicked laugh and closed the door on her unwanted visitors.

Chapter Eleven

Nina was lying in her bed thinking about how well her plan was working. After Benjamin cut off her access to their funds, she couldn't get what she needed from her regular source, so she disguised herself as a homeless person to make a score in the Cass corridor. Nina didn't like slumming in the awful place, but this time, she couldn't believe her good fortune. She was staring at a vagrant, the spitting image of JJ. At first, Nina couldn't believe her eyes and hid from the person, even though she knew it couldn't be JJ because her source told her JJ was at her office.

Nina's contact was running late so she decided to approach the woman and get her story. Nina could tell the woman was in bad shape. Her face and clothing was dirty and she smelled like she hadn't showered in weeks. Nina's mind was no longer on the hit she needed. She started formulating a plan and persuaded the woman to follow her to a seedy motel off Woodward Avenue. Nina got a room and told the lady to stay put while she went to get them some food.

Nina went to the closest Coney Island, ordered breakfast and rushed back to the motel.

After they finished eating she told the woman to go take a shower. Nina peeped at the woman's clothes size and left the hotel once more. She returned with three outfits, a nightgown, slippers, and underclothes from the Salvation Army, and personal items she had picked up from the drug store for the look-alike. She returned to the room, and the stranger was wrapped in the dingy motel towel. Nina put the old clothes in the trash and handed the woman the items purchased for her. The woman put on her new-to-her clothes.

"Okay, now that you're settled what's your name?"

"Janice."

"Hi, Janice, I'm Nina." Nina offered her hand and the woman shyly accepted the handshake.

"Where are you from, Janice?" Nina needed to get as much information from Janice as possible.

"Here in Detroit." Janice spoke so softly Nina could hardly hear her.

"Do you have any family here?"

"No."

"Where do you live, Janice?"

"I don't live anywhere."

"Where did you use to live?"

"I don't want to talk about that."

"Okay. Can you tell me something about yourself?"

"What do you want with me?"

"What do you mean, Janice?"

"Why are you being so nice to me?"

"I just wanted to help you out. You seem like a nice person."

"I don't believe you."

"Look, I don't have that much money, but for some reason you touched my heart and I wanted to help you."

"I can't afford to stay here."

"Don't worry about that, Janice."

They started silently at one another before Janice got up and moved to the other side of the room.

"What do you want from me, Nina?"

"Why do you keep insisting I want something from you?"

"Because, I don't think you're from the streets."

"What makes you say that, Janice?"

"The way you speak and the way you carry yourself."

"Since we're being honest, I don't think you from the streets either. So what's your story?"

Janice hung her head. Quietly, she revealed that she had lost her job and apartment due to a gambling addiction.

"Thanks for being honest with me, Janice. I know what it's like to fall onto hard times." Nina scratched her arms and rubbed her nose repeatedly. "I have to go, but first, I'm going to get you some more food. What would you like for me to bring you back?"

Janice told Nina what she wanted. Nina returned with the food, telling Janice the only thing she expected of her was to stay in the room and not go anywhere. Nina promised to bring Janice food every day.

Nina didn't know how she was going to take care of Janice and keep up her habit. She'd already spent all the money she had. She'd have to sell her jewelry. It didn't matter to Nina. That was a small price to pay to teach JJ a lesson.

JJ and Lewis were out of their minds with worry over Leo. There had been no contact from the kidnappers to request a ransom. All they could do was rely on local authorities. JJ knew Erica and their team was working day and night searching for Leo. The Simmons family was also very supportive. Emily told Lewis not to worry about work and to stay home with JJ. Randy had put as many officers on the case as possible, but every lead they followed ended in a dead end.

JJ was distraught. She knew from working cases like this that time wasn't on their side. Studies showed child abduction cases by non-family abductors usually ended in homicides within the first three hours. The authorities had already put out an Amber alert and a BOLO (be on the lookout) to surrounding agencies.

JJ and Lewis made an emotional televised plea, offering a one hundred-thousand-dollar reward for Leo's safe return. Media outlets aired the message for several days. Most of the reward money was put up by the Simmons family and Arlene.

"Erica, do you think we're going to find Leo alive?" JJ sat at her dining room table, biting her fingernails. She was a mess. She wore an old sweat suit with no makeup. Her eyes were puffy from crying.

"JJ," Erica grabbed her friend's hands to rescue whatever nails were left. Don't give up. We'll find Leo and make sure whoever took him is punished to the fullest extent of the law."

"Come on, Erica. We all know Nina's crazy behind is involved in this up to her neck." JJ pounded the table to show her frustration. "I know one thing if we don't get any answers soon I'm going over there and beat the shit out of her until she tells me where she's holding my baby."

"JJ, I know it's hard, but we have to stay calm. We have a lot of help and Nina's dad will be home tomorrow so hopefully he'll be able to get some answers out of her." Calvin got up from the table and gave JJ a hug.

"I still don't get it. I want to blame the daycare, but the woman looked just like me. How could something like that happen?"

95

"I know. I have reviewed the tape so many times, and if you weren't with me, I would've thought it was you too." Erica didn't like that they had hardly made any progress in the case.

"My biggest fear is that we're dealing with a psycho since we haven't received a ransom demand. Lewis said.

"Baby, we have to keep praying that we get him back soon. He's just so little. I don't know what I'm going to do if we don't get him back alive and well. Nina may be crazy, but she's smart. The detail they have on her hasn't been able to come up with anything to connect her to the kidnapping, I still feel like she's involved though." JJ said.

"Guys, I have to meet Uncle Eric." Calvin stood to leave. "He has a few contacts at the FBI that may be able to look at this on the down low. I'll check with you all later."

"I'm going to leave you ladies to talk." Lewis hugged JJ and headed for their bedroom.

"He's trying to be strong for me, but I know he's having a really hard time. He keeps going off to the bedroom to be alone, and he hasn't really talked to anyone but Lance… (Lance was Lewis' best friend)." JJ's voice trailed off like she was deep in thought. Reaching up to wipe an errant tear, she added, "We were so blessed to have Leo after the miscarriage. I don't know how we're going to survive if something bad happens to our baby."

"Let's not think that way, JJ. We're going to pull out all the stops and get Leo back. I know it's not good to say or think, but since we haven't received a ransom call then whoever took Leo needs him alive. We still have a chance to move in on the assailant(s)."

JJ nodded and stood. "I'll be okay, Erica. You need to get back to the office and keep an eye on things. I'm going to check on Lewis and work from home. I need something to keep me busy."

JJ walked Erica to the door and headed upstairs to check on her husband.

Chapter Twelve

Nina was relaxing in her bedroom after taking a hit. The alcohol stopped being enough for her long ago, but the cocaine hit the spot. She had been lazing around all morning. She was so glad her dad would be out of town for another few weeks. Having the house to herself gave her the freedom to relax and get high anytime she wanted. She still couldn't believe things had gone off exactly as she planned. She couldn't wait to have Janice do more JJ movements.

Nina knew Janice didn't know anything about JJ, and Nina had no intentions of telling her. When she put her plan in motion she had helped Janice out so much that Janice had no choice but to do whatever Nina wanted her to do. It took a little while for Nina to convince Janice to take Leo, but Nina promised no harm would come to the baby and showed Janice the safe cover she had for both her and Leo, Janice agreed to Nina's outrageous plan. The trickiest part of the plan was going from place to place to get homeless people to buy baby supplies. Nina was very careful so none of this would be traced back to her.

Once Nina was fully stocked with everything she needed she had Janice go pick up Leo from the daycare as bold as day. Everything went off without a hitch. The daycare didn't think twice about releasing Leo. Even though she had been mad at first, Nina was thankful her children were gone. Their absence gave her the opportunity to come up with this plan. She knew Janice would come in handy to use against JJ eventually. When JJ refused to drop the case after Nina went and personally asked her to, she set this plan in motion. She didn't want to involve an innocent child, but she had to knock the witch down a peg or two. All JJ had to do was drop the case.

Nina would protect Leo from harm, but she had no intentions of giving him back until she received full custody of her children, and Benjamin was getting on her last nerve trying to persuade her to check herself into rehab, and come clean about Leo's disappearance. She knew she was under surveillance so she would let them see only what she wanted them to see. The tricky part of the plan was getting Janice and Leo into the panic room. Nina was sure her dad forgot all about this room, so even if he were at home, her plan would still work. She would have to be careful once he returned home, but that would be a piece of cake. Nina was proud of herself for sneaking Leo and Janice into the house tucked away in a shipment box. The people on her tail wouldn't know she or her father had not received an actual delivery.

Nina decided to run a few errands. She would clean the house later. The friends she had over last night made a mess. She wished the housekeeper was there to clean, but Nina didn't want her to see the mess. She sat up in the bed, stretched, and headed to the bathroom to take a shower. Once dressed, she went downstairs. The sound of someone opening the front door with a key threw her into panic mode. Nina grabbed an umbrella. It was the first thing she saw sitting in the corner. Her dad walked in, Nina's cloudy mind couldn't figure out what to do next.

"Daddy, what are you doing here?" Nina grabbed her chest like she was having a heart attack.

"Hello to you too, Nina. If I remember correctly, I live here."

"I'm sorry. I just meant…I wasn't expecting you for another few weeks." Nina returned the umbrella to the corner. How in the hell would she explain the mess around the house?

"I decided to cut my trip short."

"I would have picked you up from the airport if I'd known you were coming home."

"I managed." Nathan headed towards the stairs then stopped abruptly and went into the living room.

Looking at the mess, her dad bellowed. "What the hell have you been doing while I was away, Nina, and where is Rosa?"

"Daddy, I'll clean this mess up. Rosa wanted to spend time with her family so I gave her some time off."

"This is unacceptable, Nina. I'm going to take a shower and when I come back down, I want this mess cleaned up and we're going to have a long talk." Nathan stormed up the stairs and slammed his bedroom door.

Arlene sat at her desk working on an acquisition, though she was finding it difficult to concentrate. In a few minutes, she would be meeting one-on-one with Samuel who was still having a hard time accepting Arlene and Cedric's engagement. The last time the three of them had dinner together it was tense. Arlene thought it was progress that Sam had at least made an appointment to meet with her and not just dropped in like he'd done in the past. She had no idea what Samuel wanted to talk about, but she had every intention of putting him in his place once and for all, because her relationship with Cedric was too important to her.

Arlene wanted to be able to tell Emily everything was under control. Arlene had to admit to herself that she was a little worried too. Samuel seemed hell bent on breaking her and Cedric up. His behavior wasn't normal at all and she was at a disadvantage because Sam knew so much about her entire life from her time in therapy. The knock on the door startled Arlene out of her morbid thoughts. Sam walked in, and Arlene found it hard to take her eyes off him. He was such a handsome man. On the outside, he was better looking than Cedric even though they had similar features. Cedric had more of a giving heart and a better personality than his brother.

Arlene had no desire to be alone with Samuel any longer than she had to.

"What brings you by today, Sam?"

"Direct as ever I see. I'm here to talk about Cedric."

"What about him?"

"Arlene, I tried to advise you that it isn't the right time for you to get involved in a serious relationship."

"I took your advisement under consideration and thought differently."

"I don't want to see my brother get hurt."

"What makes you think I'm going to hurt him?"

"We both know your history with men, Arlene."

"That's private and confidential and shouldn't be brought up since I'm no longer in therapy. I don't like the fact that you're using my past against me, Sam."

"I'm not using it against you. I'm just saying that you need to completely heal before jumping into another marriage."

"I'm done talking about this, Sam. I've discussed my past with Cedric and we're fine. I WILL NOT talk to you about this again."

Samuel stood. The crazed look in his eyes scared the daylights out of Arlene. The look was there and gone so quickly, Arlene almost wondered if she had imagined it. Samuel smiled at her, said his goodbyes and walked out the door. Arlene put her head on her desk relieved to be alone again.

Chapter Thirteen

Nathan stalled going back downstairs. He was so disappointed in Nina. She looked like she'd been on a binge since he left which confirmed his decision to arrange an intervention as soon as possible. He knew getting Nina to return to the home she shared with Benjamin wasn't going to be easy, but she was at a point where she had to indulge Nathan's request. Nina did not like it when he was upset or disappointed in her. Nathan could hear Nina moving around downstairs and this angered him even more. The total disrespect she had for his home was unreal. There was no telling what else she'd been doing while he was away and to be truthful he didn't want to know.

Nathan had spent part of the time he was away trying to find help for his daughter. Since he didn't have a legal right to have her committed, the next best thing was an intervention and finding an intervention specialist that would work with them on short notice was difficult. The normal prep time had to be by-passed because if Nina had anything to do with Leo's disappearance, time was of the essence. Once the specialist was in place, forming the group of people to speak to Nina was less stressful. Nathan knew emotions would be on high alert since the participants in the group didn't have time to prepare for a successful intervention. Even though skipping the planning stage of the intervention process was risky, they had to work within the limited time frame. Thankfully, after Nathan explained the dire circumstances to the specialist, he agreed.

The intervention group would consist of: Nathan, Benjamin, family doctor (Julie Westbrook), intervention specialist (Dennis Albertson), Benjamin's mother Beth, his sister Lyn, JJ, Erica, and Benjamin. They were meeting at Benjamin's house at four o'clock. At one point, Nathan and Benjamin thought about asking Randy to attend, but Nathan didn't want to put Nina in an even bigger state of denial. The group was prepared for Nina's anger. When Benjamin called and asked his mom to come home for the intervention, she wanted no part of it, but he convinced her it would be in the best interest of the children. Lyn didn't want to be there either. She never liked Nina and didn't have anything good to say about her except she was grateful for her nephew and niece. JJ most definitely didn't want to be there, but she felt she might be able to get answers about Leo's disappearance in this formal setting.

Nathan went downstairs. Nina had cleaned the house spotless, changed her clothes and put on makeup. She looked more like his self-confident daughter, but Nathan knew this was just for show and that his daughter needed immediate help. He prayed she didn't have anything to do with the kidnapping, but in his heart, he knew she was involved. He asked her to sit so they could talk, and, Nina did so with a hesitant look in her eyes.

"Nina, I'm worried about you."

"Daddy, I'm fine. As matter of fact, I've been looking for work."

Nathan knew Nina was lying. "That's good, Nina, but we still need to address the issues you need to work on before you become employed."

"I told you before. I don't have any issues, Dad. What more do you want from me? I moved in here so we could work on our relationship and for me to get my life together while the children are away. I'm sorry I let the house get a little messy."

"I know, Nina." Nathan switched gears. He couldn't push Nina any further without giving away his intentions. "I need you to make a run with me for a few hours. Are you free?"

"Sure, Daddy. We haven't done the father/daughter thing in a long time. Maybe we could go shopping and grab a bite to eat while we're out."

Nathan grabbed his keys.

"We'll see." He held the door open for his daughter and they left the house.

After ten minutes of driving, Nathan told Nina they needed to stop by Benjamin's house for a few minutes. She told her dad she didn't like the idea, but she would be okay if it was just a few minutes. Nathan was glad Benjamin remembered to tell everyone to park elsewhere. They pulled into the driveway, and Nathan asked Nina to come inside with him. Nina was reluctant, but finally gave in. Nathan used the new key Benjamin had given him after having the locks changed once Nina moved out. Nathan and Nina walked in, greeted by everyone seated around the dining room table waiting for them. Nina immediately became hostile.

"What the hell is going on here?" Nina's voice was low and menacing.

Nathan had a slight hold on his daughter's arm. "We're all here to address your problems, Nina. We're concerned about you."

"How could you do this to me, Dad?"

"Nina…honey, I know you think I've betrayed you, but you have problems that need to be addressed." Nathan had a sad look on his face.

Nina looked around and then back at her dad. "And I'm supposed to think everyone in this room has my best interest at heart? I know none of you give a damn about me."

Dr. Westbrook got up from the table to comfort Nina. She explained that no one wanted to hurt her. They were just concerned about her well-being.

"No," Nina shook her head furiously. "Everyone just wants to gang up on me and blame me for shit that's not my fault." She looked at JJ, "I'm sorry about your baby, JJ, but I had nothing to do with his disappearance. And as for you, Ben, haven't you destroyed my life enough?"

109

A man stood and approached Nina with his hand extended. "Nina, my name is Dennis Albertson. I'm here to assist you and your family and friends through this process."

"I don't have any friends here, and as far as family there's only my dad. But, I can see he's turned against me too." Nina said, defiantly.

"You're wrong, Nina. Your dad loves you very much and everyone in this room cares enough about you to get you help."

"I guess this is the part where everyone in the room gets to put me down."

"Not put you down, but they are here to express how what you're going through may be affecting their lives."

"Look, Dennis, I told my dad I have everything under control so this is a waste of my time." Nina turned to leave, and Benjamin spoke up.

"Nina, I've tried to do my best by you, but the more I try to help you the worse off you become. I know we are getting a divorce, but I still care about you. Our children need you to be whole again, so please for their sake listen to what we have to say and get help."

"Stop it, right damn now! Every time you want to control me you use my children. That's the main reason I want them away from your sorry ass." Nina yelled.

"Yeah, well that's not going to happen. But here's what's going to happen. If you don't get help, I will file an order so you won't have any access to them. You are a danger to our children and to yourself." Benjamin snapped back.

"You bastard, I hate you and I hope you rot in hell." Nina made a move toward Benjamin, but Dennis and Dr. Westbrook stopped her.

Benjamin's mom, Elizabeth spoke up. "Nina, I know we've had our problems over the last few years, but for the children's sake please take care of yourself. They love you and they need you in their lives."

Nina rolled her eyes. "Beth, don't pretend you're on my side. You turned against me and believed everything that son of yours told you."

Dennis motioned for Benjamin's sister, Evelyn to speak next.

"Look you know I'm going to keep it real. I don't like you, but my brother loved you and you gave him two beautiful children we all love, so if you don't care about your sorry life, think about how what you do affects them."

"Lyn, you're nothing but a spoiled brat that should have gotten your ass beat a long time ago. Your family lets you get away with everything and you think the world owes you something. Well, I have news for you, little girl. I don't owe you a damn thing. What you say, think, or feel makes no difference to me."

Dennis and Dr. Westbrook managed to get Nina to sit. Dennis motioned for Nathan to speak.

"Baby girl, you have to know how much you mean to me. You are the last part I have of your mom. I want you to be whole again. Please heed what we're telling you."

Nina looked at her dad, with tears in her eyes. The balloon seemed to have deflated from her anger. "Daddy, I trusted you, and you brought me here to be ambushed. How am I supposed to believe you care about me?"

Dennis slightly touched Nathan's hand and gave him a subtle headshake to keep him from responding. Next, he nodded towards Calvin.

"Nina, I've only know of you through Benjamin's case. I just want to make sure my sister and JJ's safety aren't at risk. I hope things turn out well for you."

Nina started clapping, and everyone in the room had a bewildered look on their face.

"Good speech, counselor. Save your pity for someone who needs it. I don't, so stop wasting your time."

Dennis nodded towards Erica.

"I want to keep this real just like Lyn. I believe you're responsible for the pictures that both JJ and I received. That was cruel for anyone to do to children. You're a mom. Think about how that would have upset your children. I just pray you didn't have anything to do with Leo's kidnapping."

"I don't need you to tell me how to feel. You need to think about your line of work and how what you do invades people's lives. I came to your office and requested politely for you to drop this case so I could try to work something out with this fool, but you tooted your nose up in the air and ignored me." Nina was agitated.

Dennis stopped the intervention for a minute to give her an opportunity to calm down then told JJ to speak. He wanted to leave her for last. From the information he gathered Nina was most upset with her.

"Nina, you've had problems long before Ben hired my company. I'm not going to let you dictate what clients I work with now or in the future. The things you did to Erica and I with those pictures was child's play. But if you're responsible for my son's disappearance, there isn't a hole you can crawl under that I won't find you. I'll hunt you down like the rabid dog you are." JJ had tears in her eyes.

Before anyone could stop her, Nina jumped up and smacked JJ across the face. JJ trained to defend herself had Nina in a chokehold so tight it took Calvin, Erica, and Benjamin to break the ladies apart.

After Nina caught her breath, she said to JJ. "Bitch, I hope your crazy ass never get your brat back. Wherever the hell he is, he's better off far away from you."

"Cut it out, Nina." Nathan had never seen this side of Nina and knew for sure she needed professional help.

He asked Dr. Westbrook and Dennis if he or Benjamin could commit her to a facility. They both told him no. JJ said she would press assault charges against Nina if she didn't sign herself into a facility immediately and take a drug test. Seeing that she didn't have a choice, Nina agreed to sign herself into a facility for seventy-two hours of observation. Before leaving with Dr. Westbrook, Dennis, and her dad, Nina told JJ she had made the biggest mistake of her life and with a crazy laugh they took Nina away.

Chapter Fourteen

To appease her dad and that bitch JJ, Nina had to agree to outpatient therapy. For an undetermined amount of time, she would attend AA meetings followed by therapy sessions. Nina hated going through all of this, but knew she couldn't afford to be committed to a facility. She had to take care of Janice and Leo. It was already hard to check on them with her dad watching her like a hawk. He had even hired extra staff so there was someone around the house twenty-four/seven. Nina dressed early and crept down to the basement's secret room to check on her guests.

"Nina, I've got to get out of here, I'm going stir crazy." Janice looked one hundred percent different than the homeless lady Nina found living on the streets. Sometimes Nina had to control her anger and remember Janice wasn't JJ.

"Isn't having a warm place to stay and food in your belly better than the life you used to live?"

"I appreciate all you've done for me, but I don't know how to take care of a baby. He cries a lot and I can't get much sleep."

"Now you're whining like a baby. I took you off the streets and gave you a better life.

Things are not going to be like this forever. I just need a little more time to think about my next move."

"How does the baby play a part in all of this? I was so nervous picking him up. All I could think about was the police arresting me for kidnapping."

"Well, you see that didn't happen, so chill out."

"How can I chill out? You won't tell me anything about your plan, especially the part where I can just walk into a daycare I've never been in before and walk out with a baby without anyone questioning why?"

"I will tell you what you need to know when you need to know it. I just wanted to make sure you guys were okay. Do you need anything?"

"Answers. You need to tell me what's going on when you come back this afternoon or I will have to find out for myself."

"Are you threatening me, Janice?"

"No, Nina. I know better than to do that. I'm just saying I want to know what's going on now rather than later."

"I have to go. Take care of that baby, and I'll see you this afternoon." Nina left the secret room and wondered how much longer she was going to be able to put Janice off. Although the room was equipped with a half bath, space for a changing table, and a small wardrobe, Nina understood why Janice was restless. It was a bonus that the room was soundproof.

JJ and Lewis decided one of them had to go back to work. Since Emily said he could have all the time he needed, JJ decided to get back to business. She hadn't slept a full night since Leo was abducted. She had prayed the intervention would lead them to her son, but it didn't work out that way. JJ wished she had beat the shit out of Nina for slapping her, but once she calmed down she realized if Nina was gone she might not ever find her son. Ben offered again for them to drop his case, but now it was a moot point.

After reviewing the case more thoroughly, Erica and JJ realized Nina or whoever slipped those pictures into the classrooms had to know someone on staff. It was frustrating that the school was no closer to finding out how any of this happened.

"I need a break." Erica said, massaging her shoulders. "How hard do you think it's going to be to find bridesmaid dresses for Auntie Arlene's wedding?"

"I don't know, but it will be interesting. JJ smiled. "Your mom is working so hard planning this wedding. If it doesn't come off without a hitch, she is going to have a fit."

Erica laughed. "I know, and Auntie is so happy I'm really happy for her, but I'm a little worried about Samuel's behavior. I don't know what the heck is wrong with him."

"It's spooky. I hope we're not going to have a stalker situation on our hands. The last thing we need right now is another high profile case." JJ shuddered, thinking about how the Simmons family would react if something happened to Arlene.

"I'm still a little concerned about Auntie Delores too. My mom and aunts are cordial, but that's about it. They were hesitant to include her in the wedding planning. I guess I just don't understand their lack of trust after all this time." Erica confided.

"You know how protective they are of Eric. I was blessed not to get the third degree since it took so long for us to solve Arlene's hit-and-run case."

"Well, I for one told Uncle Eric up front you were part of the family even though you guys weren't together. You are important to all of us, JJ, so you have no worries."

"Thank you, Erica. You guys are important to me too. I just wish I had more family.
Sometimes I feel so alone in the world. I love you guys and Lewis, but not having any biological family other than Leo is really hard to deal with at times."

"Have you ever thought about searching for your birth family?"

"No. My parents were my family and that's all I need to know. I was devastated when I found out they adopted me and had no intentions of telling me." JJ's dad died when she was a teenager. Ten years ago, on her deathbed, her mom told JJ she was adopted, but the adoption wasn't legal. JJ didn't understand what her mom meant by that, and unfortunately, her mom passed before she could get any more details.

"You know they couldn't tell you since your adoption weren't legal. Oh my God! I don't know why I didn't think of this before. Wait a minute, that stranger that walked off with Leo what if she was part of your birth family like a sister or twin or something?"

"You know what…That would make so much sense." JJ had a frown on her face while she thought about this new scenario.

"I feel like we're getting somewhere now. Let me call Lewis. I'll have him bring my mom's boxes down from the attic. I'm so glad I kept all that stuff. After she passed away I was tempted to throw all of it away so I wouldn't have to deal with the fact that my whole life had been a lie."

"JJ, I can't imagine how all of this feels. It would blow my mind if I was to find out my family wasn't really my biological family.

"I have a better idea. Since things are under control here, do you want to come home with me?" JJ asked. "We can work on going through my mom's things from there and it will give me a chance to check on Lewis."

"Sure." Erica said. "I'll meet you there in an hour. I want to stop by the school and check on the twins."

Erica and JJ wrapped up what they were doing at the office and left to take care of business.

Chapter Fifteen

Arlene sat at the table in the back of Antonio's with Emily and Erin waiting on Delores.

The ladies were meeting for lunch to go over Arlene's wedding plans and to discuss what was going on in the family.

"Why does Delores have to be so bossy?" Erin sighed heavily.

"Erin, are you still pouting about Eric's relationship with Delores? There haven't been any problems between them in years." Arlene scolded. "You promised to work on behaving yourself."

"I have been behaving myself. I just don't care much for that woman."

"She's not so bad. Just think about how peaceful our brother's life is right now. Or I should say was until this mess with Benjamin's case came up."

"You right, ladies." Erin squeezed her sister's hand and nodded at Arlene. Just as she picked up her cup to take another sip, Delores came in and took the vacant seat next to Arlene.

"Hi, ladies, what did I miss?"

"Nothing. We were waiting for you before we started discussing the wedding." Emily spoke up before Erin said something crazy.

"Okay. Let's order. I'm starving." Delores said.

JJ and Erica decided to have a quick lunch before tackling the boxes Lewis retrieved from the attic. She wanted to do more research before she told Lewis about the new angle they were considering in the case.

JJ didn't know whether to be happy or sad about the possibility of having other family members out there. If she did have a sister or twin why would she want to take her baby? Wouldn't she want to contact JJ instead of punishing her by taking her child?

Lewis decided to go into the office for a little while since JJ was going to be at home. JJ had a crying and screaming fit to get rid of some of her pain and frustration. Walking back into her house and not seeing her baby tore her apart, especially after seeing the sad look on her husband's face. JJ had more experience dealing with tough cases and loss because of her line of work, but Lewis was finding it difficult to understand why someone would take their child.

Crying helped. JJ went to wash her face and finish putting together the light lunch she was preparing for her and Erica. At the sound of the doorbell, she wiped her hands on a towel and went to answer the door.

Erica could tell JJ had been crying again and pulled her friend into a hug before they went into the kitchen to eat. Bellies nourished, they went into the den where Lewis had left all the boxes. JJ was glad the boxes were labeled to save time.

"Are you sure you're ready for this?" Concern laced Erica's inquiry. "I can go through these if you want to get a little rest." Erica gently touched one of the bags underneath JJ's eye.

JJ grimaced and grabbed Erica's hand, squeezing it slightly. "No, but thanks for the offer, I have to deal with this sooner or later. If we're able to find a connection to what happened to my baby, I would search through a hundred boxes."

"I thought about it on the way over here. What if Nina or someone else found out you had family members out there you didn't know about? It could very well be someone from an old case that has a grudge against you."

"That's true, but my gut is telling me it's Nina. That chick is crazy. She swore up and down I was trying to come between her and Ben."

"Unfortunately, somebody dealing with her type of issues won't listen to reason when you try to tell them the truth. All they hear is whatever negative vibe going on in their heads."

"It has to be the drugs and alcohol or whatever she's on controlling her because she checked out of their marriage a long time ago according to her and Ben."

"I was trying to figure out why a family member would work with someone to bring you down. Have you had any strangers approach you or attempt to get in touch with you recently?"

JJ shook her head. "No, I haven't and I've went over my old cases where I thought someone might want revenge, but I couldn't come up with anyone…unless it has something to do with the prank calls Lewis been receiving."

"I agree with you. Nina is involved somehow. I didn't think that way for sure until after the intervention. I know she felt betrayed by everyone there, but I had the feeling she was angry at you the most."

"I know, and that doesn't make any sense to me. It seems like it would be Ben or her dad that she would be the most upset with not me."

"Well, if we want to find out why, I guess it's time we tackle these boxes and hope for a lead that will answer our questions."

As soon as Lewis walked through the door of his office, he knew it was a mistake to come to work. He just had to leave home so he didn't breakdown in front of JJ and Erica. He didn't know how much longer he could go on without knowing the fate of his son. JJ seemed to hold it together better than he and he wondered how she was doing it. None of this made sense to him. Usually, when a child was taken a ransom demand followed, but it had been a week since Leo was taken and they hadn't received one ransom request. How in the world could someone looking so much like JJ come in and walk out with their baby? JJ kept saying Nina is behind all of this, but Nina didn't take Leo. She and JJ didn't look anything alike. Lewis was deep in his thoughts until the commotion outside his door roused him. He went to check it out.

"What's going on out here?" Lewis was glad Emily wasn't there because she didn't go for that kind of mess in her place of business.

"Sorry, Lewis, a homeless man dropped something off for you, but he ran out of here when I tried to question him." Sherry, the office intern explained.

"What was the big deal?"

"He demanded to see you and when I asked if he had an appointment, he became belligerent."

"Just give me what he left and get back to work please."

Sherry picked up the box like it was a piece of trash and handed it to Lewis. Lewis took the dirty box into his office and sat it on his desk. He could understand why Sherry didn't want to touch it.

Lewis opened the box and screamed. "Noooooo."

Emily, who had just returned, and Sherry, came running into the office. Emily went over to his desk and peeked in the box. There were baby clothes inside.

"Those are the clothes Leo had on the last day he was at daycare." Lewis sounded distant. Emily told him not to touch anything and called Randy, Erica, and JJ. All three of them arrived at the office within twenty minutes.

JJ ran over and embraced Lewis while Randy and Erica donned gloves and inspected the box. The box held a two-piece outfit, tee shirt, booties, and a note. The note was typed and brief: *The baby is unharmed.*

"There must be something else in there. Check again, please." JJ demanded.

"Sorry, JJ. That's all that was in there. I'll take this to the lab and have everything analyzed. Randy asked the intern for a description of the man who dropped off the box and to recount everything that happened when he came in. He left with the box and the others retired to Emily's office for more privacy.

Chapter Sixteen

Nina sat in the secret room with Janice and Leo. Today was the holiday where independence was celebrated, and she felt good about how things were shaping up. She saw JJ over the weekend from afar and was happy that she looked worse for the wear. Every time she had to attend a class or counseling session, Nina hated JJ more. It didn't help that Janice had her face. The more she looked at Janice; Nina was amazed at how two people could look so much alike and yet be so different. Even though Janice was homeless she had a serene nature. JJ was arrogant, rude, and downright unlikable. She knew the heifer was lying when she said her and Benjamin never had an affair. Nina wasn't going to be satisfied until she chased JJ's husband away. Taking her son wasn't enough. She wanted JJ to know what it felt like to lose everything.

At one point, she was going to destroy her business, but decided it would hurt JJ worse to lose her family. Besides, Nina thought it would have been harder to try to destroy her business.

Janice was still bugging the shit out of her to get some air. Nina knew she was still being watched like a hawk so she couldn't take a chance on letting Janice out. It was becoming more difficult to procure baby products. Getting everything in paper bags wasn't the problem. Finding bums to buy baby products for her was the problem. They had the nerve to get greedy. She most definitely wasn't going to use that fool who dropped the clothes off again. When he told her about the scene, she beat him for five minutes straight for being so damn stupid. All he had to do was drop off the box, not ask to see anyone.

Nina used the time between her classes and her therapy sessions to make these exchanges. It was the only time the fools that were watching her didn't know what she was doing.

Nina had to hurry with the next step in her plan because it was getting harder and harder to keep Janice from being restless. Janice was more comfortable with the baby and had grown attached to him. Nina wondered how Janice would feel if she found out Leo was her nephew. The last time she and Janice had a confrontation, she almost let Janice's relation to Leo slip. Nina knew it was only a matter of time before JJ or Erica put two and two together and find out about JJ's biological family. Nina had used her dad's name to gain the confidential information.

Although JJ's adoption was illegal, Nina was able to find out about JJ's adoptive parents, and that her biological teenage mother had been a victim of rape and didn't know who the twins' dad were. The broker separated the twins because he could get more selling them individually. He had arranged for the twins' mom to deliver at home with a midwife so there would be no hospital record of the births. Unfortunately, the twins' mom encountered problems at childbirth and died a few hours later.

Janice yelled Nina's name, interrupting her trance.

"What the hell you doing all that yelling for, I'm sitting right here?" Nina said angrily.

"I called your name several times and you didn't respond. Why do you zone out like that? This isn't the first time you've done this when you are with me."

"I don't have time for your stupid questions. When I come back tonight, I'll have the next phase of my plan ready to be carried out. It won't be long before I can let you go on your merry way."

"I can't wait. You're still going to give me the agreed upon amount?"

"We have a deal, Janice, and you've kept your part, I'll do the same." Nina didn't know where she was going to get the fifty thousand dollars she promised Janice, but she would think of something. She had already sold most of her jewelry. Even though she would be glad to get rid of Benjamin, she didn't want to part with her wedding rings. She did have her divorce settlement coming, but not in the timeframe in which she promised to pay Janice. There was the reward money, but Nina couldn't figure out how to collect it without exposing herself and holding onto the baby.

"I'm going to miss this little fellow when this is all over. Is his mom doing any better?"

Nina had lied to Janice and told her they were hiding Leo from his abusive dad while his mom was in the hospital. "Yes, she's getting better every day. I'll be back with your holiday meal and all the trimmings." She smiled as she left the room, the stories she came up with were pure genius.

JJ was at her wit's end. She wondered if the day could get any worse. After Randy left to have the contents of the box analyzed, they went into the small conference room to wait for Eric and Calvin to join them. The search through her mom's things hadn't turned up anything useful except the name of the man they traced as the broker of the illegal adoption. The man had been in his fifties at the time of JJ's birth. Even if he was still alive, JJ doubted he would be able to help them. Erica had told JJ she wasn't going to give up. She would follow the lead and see if anything turned up.

Eric and Calvin walked into the conference room. Eric greeted JJ with a hug. When he released her, JJ looked at Lewis and knew by the look on her husband's face, Eric had held on longer than Lewis was comfortable with. She cleared her throat.

"Did you find anything useful in your mom's belongings?" Eric asked JJ as he took a seat.

"Oh my gosh. Wait a minute. I can't believe I forgot about mom's safe deposit box at the bank. Maybe we can find something in there." JJ said.

134

"Babe, your mom been gone for ten years. You never checked to see what she had in her safe deposit box?" Lewis asked.

JJ shook her head. "No, I was and still am angry with them for keeping secrets from me.

Erica, do you mind going with me to the bank? I have to go home to get the key and the paperwork giving me access. After the bank verifies everything, I'll let them know you will remove the contents." JJ rubbed her arms as if she were cold. "I don't know if I can handle what's in there. You can get the contents and bring it to the office. I will meet you back there." JJ didn't feel like doing anything but sleep, but she was afraid to do that for too long.

"Sure," Erica said. We can leave right now. Guys, I'll keep you posted on any new information we uncover. Lewis, hang in there." Erica squeezed Lewis's shoulder as she and JJ left the conference room.

Emily reached over and grabbed Lewis's hand. "I so sorry we can't do more to help out.

You've been my rock here at the office for years. I feel like I should be doing more to help you."

"Boss lady, you've been a big help." Lewis squeezed Emily's hand. "I really appreciate you giving me time off and your family putting up the reward money for Leo's ransom. When I walked in this morning, I thought being here was a mistake. But it seems like that man was waiting for me to return to work."

"This plan was well thought out." Calvin said. "It seems like this person is everywhere and knows what is going on all the time. If this is Nina, I'm not sure how she is pulling all of this off right under our noses. She has to have others working with her because she is being watched carefully."

"Well, we all know how smart crazy people can be." Emily shuddered.

"Even smart people make mistakes and overplay their hands. Rica is good at what she does. She'll get to the bottom of this." Eric said

"Let's go get a bite to eat while we're waiting to hear back from Erica and JJ." Emily wasn't hungry, but thought it was a good idea to get Lewis out of the office.

136

Chapter Seventeen

Erica made her way back to the office. She saw JJ's car in the parking lot, but JJ was nowhere to be found. Erica waited about fifteen minutes before going into the small conference room, to give JJ some space.

Before she left the bank, she had asked the bank manager for a security bag so she could put whatever was in the box in the bag. Once the manager returned, Erica looked into the box and knew everything would fit. The first thing she pulled out was a diary followed by a jewelry box, and a thick stack of papers. Now back at the office in the conference room, she pulled the jewelry box out. She opened it, and it played a pretty melody that she didn't recognize. Erica was amazed at the beautiful jewelry inside the box, particularly, a diamond encrusted broach that sparkled like crazy. If it was real, it was worth a small fortune. Glancing at the other jewelry in the box, she knew there was nothing else in there that would help them find Leo. She put the broach back in the box and moved it to the side.

Erica wanted to wait on JJ before she went through the papers, but she didn't think JJ would mind if she went ahead. The first document was a copy of the deed to the house where JJ and Lewis lived. The next document made Erica frown. It appeared to be JJ's birth certificate, but there were four similar documents. Erica sat the paper aside and called Calvin. Twenty minutes later Calvin sat in the conference room reviewing the documents with Erica. JJ was still absent. Calvin frowned as he reviewed the documents.

"JJ has or had a twin sister, but for some reason her parents only adopted JJ." Calvin picked up another paper and quietly reviewed it.

"This is a mess, Erica. It seems, from the paperwork, JJ's parents were promised twins but was told that only JJ survived and the other twin was stillborn. Her mom must have found out later that wasn't true. I think the broker tricked JJ's parents and decided he could get more money if he split the girls up."

Erica closed her eyes. "I was afraid something like this was happening. I wonder why she hasn't approached JJ."

"JJ's mom found out the other twin survived and was looking for her, but she died before she could be found. The private investigation company she hired is located in downtown Detroit. We need to reach out to them to see what information they can give us. I know JJ may not want to get involved, but she has to because they won't be able to tell us anything if she's not there."

JJ walked in the room with a slight smile on her face.

"Who won't tell you what? What did I miss?" JJ asked quietly.

"This is everything that was in your mom's safe deposit box." Erica said.

JJ went straight to the jewelry box.

"Have you guys had a chance to review the documents?" JJ voice was as low as a whisper.

Erica looked at JJ. She wasn't used to hearing her partner whisper unless they were on surveillance.

"We have, and we were on the right track. You have a twin sister. Your parents were told that she was stillborn, but the broker separated you guys at birth. About six months before she passed, your mom found out your twin was still alive. She started searching for her, but didn't find her before she passed away." Erica never broke contact with JJ's face, paying close attention to her reaction.

JJ's face remained blank the entire time.

"What's wrong with me? If I have a twin out there why don't I feel like a part of me is missing?" This time JJ didn't try to hide her tears.

"JJ, I know this is hard for you." Erica hugged her friend. "But we have to contact the company your mom hired to find your sister. They're located in downtown Detroit, and as you know they won't release any information to us. Are you up to taking this on right now?" Erica asked.

"I have to be. I want my baby back. Why would she take him from me?" JJ wailed.

"I'm not sure, honey, but Calvin and I will be with you every step of the way. Now, let's head downtown."

Nathan decided to pay Benjamin a visit at his office. It had been a little over a week since Nina's intervention and although she was faithfully going to her meetings and therapy, he felt she wasn't getting any better. He asked the staff to keep an eye on her every move and they told him she often went down to the basement when he wasn't home. Nathan found that unusual and went down there to see what was keeping her attention. He checked the entertainment room to be sure she wasn't hiding any booze or drugs, but came up empty. He was hoping Benjamin might be able to enlighten him.

"I can't put my finger on it, but Nina is acting very strange." Nathan said, drumming his fingers on Benjamin's desk. "I haven't caught her slipping, but she is so happy with herself, sometimes it's hard to believe she's not high."

"Maybe there's a new man in her life." Benjamin offered. "I've always hoped one day when Nina was whole she would find herself a supportive mate."

Nathan shook his head. "I don't think that's it. My contact says she goes from her meetings to therapy and back home. She spends a lot of time down in the basement so I checked it to make sure she wasn't using down there."

"Sir, I feel so bad for asking JJ to take my case. I know Nina is your daughter, and I'm sorry to admit it, but I agree with Erica and JJ. Nina is somehow involved."

"My gut is telling me that too, but she's all I have left. I just need her to go back to being that sweet carefree girl of the past."

"I miss that Nina too, but I'm afraid we may never see her like that again."

"In a few weeks, you're not going to have to worry about her any longer. The healing will be over for you, but just starting for Nina. I just hope losing a husband and children won't send her over the edge."

"I have faith that Nina will pull herself together soon so she won't have to be without the children for long. Once she is better, I will work with her any way I can on co-parenting."

"That day may be a long time away. She's still denying she has a problem. I wonder why JJ's presence seems to set her on such a dangerous path of self-destruction."

"I've been trying to figure that out for the longest. And, Sir, just so you know, I've never had an affair with JJ or anyone else. Even when I knew our marriage was over, I was never unfaithful to Nina."

"That's good to hear, son. I just wished Nina had focused on something else to fill her time once the children were in school. She should've been working or doing something productive.

She told me you were generous with your settlement, and I appreciate that. I'm working on becoming her guardian."

"I think she would've been better off in a facility where she could get full-time help."

"I know, son. That's why if I'm able to get guardianship of her or power of attorney, I plan to have her committed."

"Sounds good, let me know if I can be of help."

Nathan left to spend some constructive time with Nina and hopefully get her to admit to her problems.

Chapter Eighteen

On their way to Burns and Associates, JJ apologized to Erica and Calvin for being out of sorts. She seemed to have lost all of her investigative instincts and hadn't had a clear thought since Leo's disappearance. Erica assured her there was no need to apologize. JJ finally got up enough nerve to ask Calvin about the other documents that were in her mom's safe deposit box. He told JJ there were some old letters that he didn't read because they looked personal and an updated will amendment adding her twin sister if she were ever found. JJ would keep the house, (Including the contents), but the stocks, bonds, and money would be split fifty-fifty. JJ would keep her dad's BMW and her mom's jewelry.

They arrived at Burns and Associates before he could go over anything else. Before they reached the receptionist area, Calvin told JJ she would have to initiate contact. JJ nodded and approached the receptionist.

"Hi, my name is Jasmine Jefferson. I'm here to speak to the investigator that handled my mom's case, Lucille Jefferson."

"Do you have the investigator's name, Ms. Jefferson?"

"No, I don't. My mom died ten years ago. I recently went through the contents of her safe deposit box and found out I had a twin sister she was looking for before she passed away."

"Normally you have to set up an appointment to see our investigators, but I remember your mom's case because I recently added old unresolved cases to our archives. Let me see if Mr. Burns is available. Feel free to have a seat while I check with him."

The receptionist went to the back and came out a few minutes later.

"Mr. Burns will see you now." She led the trio into Jasper Burns' office, brought in another chair and sat it in front of the big cherry oak desk before closing the door behind her.

"Your reputation precedes you, Ms. Jefferson. Even though it's been a while since your mother passed, I'm sorry for your loss." The man extended his arm toward the chairs, indicating they were welcome to have a seat. "I'm ill prepared for your unexpected visit today, Ms. Jefferson, how may I assist you?"

Jasper Burns, owner and CEO of Burns and Associates was an older Caucasian man in his late-fifties.

"I'm here about the case you started for my mom to find my twin sister."

"Well, being a private investigator yourself, you know that information is privileged."

"I understand all that, but this twin sister whom I knew nothing about before today, walked into my son's daycare and walked out with him two weeks ago. It's imperative that I know what information you found out about her because she…" JJ lost her composure as tears fell.

Erica took over the conversation while Calvin consoled JJ.

"I hope you understand the importance of this information, Mr. Burns."

I'm so sorry." Mr. Burns cleared his throat. "Excuse me while I have my assistant pull the files." Jasper left the room to speak to his assistant.

When he returned to the office, he told them Mrs. Jefferson had stopped the investigation when she became sick and informed him that JJ would be in touch with his firm after her death if she wanted to continue the case. Since they hadn't heard from JJ, no additional work had been performed.

"Mr. Burns, I don't know if JJ's mom told you, but she didn't tell JJ she was adopted until she was on her death bed. Understandably, JJ was upset and didn't go through her mother's belongings at that time."

Jasper nodded. "Please call me Jasper. May I call you Erica?"

"Sure, and this is my brother Calvin."

"Jasper, did my mom tell you why she didn't tell me I was adopted?" JJ asked.

"From what I understand, JJ, your mom and dad tried for years to have a child, but was unsuccessful. Because of your father's felony record, they couldn't go through the normal adoption channels."

"My dad was a felon? What did he do time for?" JJ was visibly surprised by this new information.

"That's public record." Jasper said. "He served eight years in prison for driving a getaway car in an attempted bank robbery. He was only twenty-two.

"Wow, I feel like I never even knew the people that raised me." JJ put her hands on top of her head. "What about my biological parents?"

Jasper hesitated.

"You have a lot going on, JJ. Why don't we just concentrate on finding your sister?"

"I'd like to know about my biological parents, Jasper." JJ shrilled.

Jasper's assistant knocked on the door and brought in a medium size box. Jasper looked through it and pulled out a file folder marked Jefferson, Lucille, CONFIDENTIAL.

"Here is all the information I came up with on your biological parents." He said handing the folder to JJ. "In a nutshell, your biological mother was raped by an unknown assailant when she was sixteen. She came from a strict background that didn't believe in abortion so her parents insisted she have the child and give it up for adoption. Your mom wanted to keep you so she ran away and kind of lived on the streets. When she was around six months pregnant she tried to go back home, but your grandparents refused to let her stay if she wouldn't give you up for adoption. She headed back to the streets and was eventually picked up by

148

this family. Long story short, they knew your mom was too young to take care of a baby and hooked her up with a baby broker. He was already working on finding a baby your parents. A few weeks later they found out your biological mom, (Valencia Young), was pregnant with twins. Your parents paid to have both of you, but the broker got greedy and decided he could get more money if you were separated. When the mid-wife delivered you and your sister he told your parents that one of you was still-born. Six months before your mom's death, she found out your twin was alive and hired our firm to find her."

"I can't believe this shit. It's like a Lifetime movie or something." JJ was pissed.

"What about my birth mom? Where is she?"

"I'm sorry, JJ." Jasper said, with a shake of his head. "She died giving birth to the two of you, unfortunately, which made it that much easier for the broker to get away with his lie. From what I discovered, he died fifteen years ago in a car accident."

"What about my birth grandparents?"

149

"They're gone too. Valencia was their only child and I couldn't find any family members on your grandparent's side of the family."

"Why would my sister take my baby? What could she possibly have against me? I don't understand why she wants to hurt someone she doesn't even know." JJ began sobbing again. Jasper reached into the box and brought out another folder.

"Here is a dossier I started on her. As you can see, I don't have any current information. She seemed to disappear after she lost her fiancé. He died from a sudden brain aneurysm a week before they were to be married.

JJ glanced at the file and handed it to Erica. Erica read quickly and passed it to Calvin.

"Looks like we have the last four years missing from where you left off. Do you have any leads like friends or anyone we can follow up with, Jasper?" Calvin asked.

Jasper shook his head no and turned his palms face up, empty handed. "Sorry, the well ran dry when she lost her apartment and her last job."

"May we have a copy of this?" Erica wanted to follow-up.

"Sure." Jasper called his assistant and asked her to make a copy of the contents in the Lucille's file.

Erica thanked Jasper and they left once they received the copy of the file.

"Guys, do you mind dropping me off at home? I'll get my car later. I can't even think straight right now." JJ said.

They entered the vehicle and headed to JJ and Lewis' home. On the way, JJ asked Calvin details about her sister. She didn't want to read what was in the file, but she was curious.

"Her name is Janice Louise Hudson. She lost her adopted parents when she was four years old. It seems they didn't want her once they were able to have their own child. She was then placed in foster care and moved from house to house where she suffered abuse and neglect. She fell in with the wrong crowd when she was a teenager, until her high school dance teacher became her mentor. In Janice's senior year, the teacher died in a plane crash, and Janice dropped out of school, started hanging out with her old crowd again, drinking and using drugs. She turned her life around when she met and fell in love with Vincent Green. She earned her GED

151

and went on to get an accounting degree from Wayne State University. After she graduated, they were engaged. But as Jasper reported, Vincent died before they could marry."

"Wow." JJ said. "She had a hard life. I wonder how she found out about me."

"This has Nina's name written all over it." Erica said. "I need you to try and get some rest. I'll assign someone to find out more about Vincent Green. Calvin will follow-up with Randy, and I will check on Nina."

JJ nodded. "Thanks guys. I'm exhausted. I'm going to try to get some sleep, but please keep me posted." JJ walked to her door. Erica waited for JJ to go inside then turned to Calvin and said, "We have to find Leo before she loses all hope of getting him back safely."

Calvin nodded as Erica backed her car out of the driveway.

Chapter Nineteen

Erica sat at her desk. Normally, she would be at home with the twins and Jonathan, but they were away for the weekend spending time with Jonathan's mom. Since leaving Nathan's house yesterday, she couldn't shake the feeling that Nina was hiding something.

Nina was nowhere to be found when she stopped by, so she and Nathan talked while he fixed them a light meal. Nathan assured Erica Nina hadn't missed any of her classes or therapy sessions. He told her about his visit with Benjamin and said he too felt Nina was hiding something thought he didn't believe his daughter would hurt Leo. Erica told Nathan about Leo's clothes being delivered to Lewis' office.

Nathan made Nina come downstairs and join them in the dining room for the meal.

Nina had launched into Erica.

"Erica, what do you want? I'm doing everything you people want and you still won't let me have any peace."

Erica didn't take the bait. Calmly, she said, "Nina, please. It's been over two weeks since Leo's disappearance. We'll let the courts know you're seeking help if you just tell us where to find him."

"How many times and in how many ways do I have to tell you people that I don't have any idea where that baby is or who has him?" Nina pounded the table.

"Nina, you and I both know that's not true." Erica insisted.

"Daddy, do I have to sit here and listen to this load of bull?"

"Nina, I love you and you know it, but I also know when you are holding something back, so please be honest with Erica. I promise to stand by your side baby girl." Nathan encouraged her.

"Thanks for the support, Dad. Nina pouted and folded her arms like a rebellious child.

"This is serious, Nina. I'm sure if you help JJ get her baby back safely, she will tell the authorities to go easy on you."

"Yeah right and my name is Tiny Tim. That hateful woman wouldn't rest until I was under the jail if I had anything to do with her brat's disappearance."

154

It had taken all of Erica's self-control not to knock the shit out of Nina for talking about Leo like that.

"Nina, where are your maternal instincts? You are a mother with two children. What if that was BJ or Brianna?" Nathan had tried to reason with his daughter.

"You should be asking her and JJ that question. Here they are hell bent on taking my children from me, and I'm supposed to care about JJ's feelings. Please." Nina folded her arms across her body and rolled her neck.

"Nina, your dad is right. We just want Leo back safe and sound. We'll help out any way we can to see that you get treatment and eventually visitation and joint custody of your children once you're well."

"For the last damn time, there isn't anything wrong with me. Leave me the hell alone." Nina jumped out of her chair and ran upstairs.

"I'm sorry, Erica. I know this visit didn't work out like you planned. Nina is being watched like a hawk. Her calls are being monitored, so I don't know how she's keeping in touch with the kidnappers."

155

Erica nodded. "Thanks for your help, Nathan, and thank you for the meal." She had been about to stand when she thought of something else. "Nathan, you said Nina only goes out for her classes and sessions, right?"

"Yes. Occasionally, she does a little shopping, but she heads straight home afterwards."

"Have you noticed her doing anything unusual when she's at home?"

"No, not really. She spends a lot of time downstairs. She calls it her sanctuary."

Erica nodded. "I see. Well, thanks again, Nathan."

Erica left Nathan's home with an uneasy feeling. She was missing something. Now sitting at her desk, she put more thought into the information they had gathered so far.

Erica's train of thought was interrupted when her cell phone rang with Benjamin on the other end.

"Good morning, Ben. What can I help you with this morning?"

"I was hoping you would be able to tell me that JJ has Leo back."

"No she doesn't.

"Erica, I'm really sorry about all of this. If I had known taking my case would bring harm to you ladies, I wouldn't have asked you guys to take it."

"It's all part of the job, Ben. I'm glad you called though. Have you talked to Nina since the intervention?"

"No, I've tried calling her twice. The first time she told me to leave her alone and the second time she told me to talk to her attorney."

"I went to see Nathan last night, and he made Nina come downstairs. She was still hostile, especially whenever JJ's name came up."

"I don't understand that, Erica. Nina and JJ didn't have any conflicts between them that I'm aware of. Out of nowhere, Nina started hating on JJ even before you guys took the case."

"Why would she think you guys were having an affair?"

"I have no idea. She has become so irrational over the last six months. The children, at times, seem like they are afraid of her. I know she won't harm them, but when she's high, her actions are unpredictable."

"I had an eerie feeling when I walked into Nathan's house last night. I can't put my finger on it, but I think the answers we're searching for are in that house."

"I don't know what that could be. I do know Nina was really upset when her dad came home unexpectedly. He said she had let the housekeeper go and the house was a mess."

"What about money? Does Nina have access to large amounts of money?"

"Not on my end she doesn't. I think Nathan pretty much cut her off too. I did forget to block her off our household account and she pretty much cleaned that account out, but there was only a few thousand dollars in there."

"How long ago was that when she took the money out?"

Benjamin was sitting in front of his computer at home so he punched in the information.

"Her last withdrawal was June seventeenth for four hundred dollars."

"That's not much with a drug and alcohol habit to support."

"Unfortunately, before I realized Nina had a real problem our wet bar used to be fully stocked. I don't know if she was able to stash anything and I know it took a while for Nathan to clear his bar too."

"I was thinking if she took Leo and had someone working with her, she has to have a way to pay them."

"Over the years, she has accumulated jewelry and other expensive items she could hock or sale if she wanted quick money."

"I thought about that. I know she didn't get rid of her wedding rings because she was wearing them last night."

"I even blocked her access to our children's educational funds. In her state of mind, I couldn't trust that she wouldn't drain those accounts."

"So, from a financial standpoint it looks like she can't afford to be frivolous with her money."

"I hope that's the case. She's been having affairs for at least a few years now so I don't know if she has money from that source."

"What can you tell me about Nathan's house?"

"He brought the house as a wedding gift for his wife, (Nina's mom) when they were first married. A year later, Nina was born and she lived there until we got married."

"What about the layout? Do you think you would be able to get that for me without Nina finding out?"

"Sure, I can ask Nathan to meet me today if he's not busy. I'll get back to you once I have it."

Erica and Benjamin wrapped up their phone call and went on to finish out their day.

Chapter Twenty

Nina seethed all weekend. Erica had a damn nerve to come check up on her and lying through her damn teeth. Nina knew Erica's statement about them helping her if Leo was returned safely was a load of bull. That woman would do or say anything to get that brat back for her friend. Nina had to refrain from going to check on Janice and Leo this weekend. Seeing Janice's face would have caused her to catch a case. She understood Janice was an innocent victim in this scenario, just as Leo was, but Nina couldn't get JJ's arrogant smug face out of her head taunting her every minute of the day.

Now, it was Monday morning and Nina was getting ready to go to that stupid class and therapy session JJ forced her into attending. Nina was ready to activate the last phase of her plan, but her dad had someone watching every move she made except when she went to the restroom and it was irritating as hell.

Nina knew she needed to check on Janice and Leo before Janice got restless and tried to leave. She and Leo had enough supplies, but Janice was ready to leave and truthfully, Nina was ready for her to go.

She'd come to like Janice and didn't understand how she could like the twin of a person she hated so much. With an hour to kill, she grabbed her dirty laundry and headed for the basement. She was surprised to see her dad sitting at the kitchen table.

"Good morning, Daddy. You're up early." Nina tried to sound cheerful, but she didn't feel that way at all.

"I've decided to go to your appointments with you today."

"Why? I know this has to do with the visit from Erica."

"I just want to see how you're progressing, Nina.

"Daddy, I had a few errands to run after my appointments." Nina had planned to sell some more jewelry so she could come up with the money she promised Janice.

"Can they wait, baby girl? I was hoping to spend some quality time with you. I miss the closeness we use to share."

"Okay, Daddy. I'll just take this back upstairs. Give me fifteen minutes and I'll be ready to go."

I'll wait for you in the car." Nathan yelled up the stairs.

Erica was anxious to search Nathan's house. She was glad Nathan told the staff not to come in today because they didn't want anyone tipping off Nina. It seemed Nina was always a step or two ahead of them, so they wanted to be very careful about their next move. Benjamin had received the call from Nathan that he would have Nina out of the house for at least four hours. They all met at the police station and rode over to Nathan's house together in an unmarked utility van. Nathan had told them to pull the van into the garage just in case someone was watching the house. He would make sure to keep Nina in sight so she wouldn't be able to make any phone calls and agreed to ask to use her phone if she had to go to the restroom or anywhere he couldn't be with her.

Randy drove around the block a few times before he felt it was safe to go to Nathan's house. He pulled into the garage and they entered the house through the back door. Benjamin told the group he would meet them in the dining room once he retrieved the floor plans Nathan had left for them. They needed a table large enough to spread out the plans. He returned to the dining room and the team looked over the plans room by room. Again, Erica got the same feeling about the house.

"I don't know guys. Everything seems straightforward, but I'm not a detective or an engineer. I'll let you all take the lead." Benjamin said.

"We have to do this carefully." Randy said, distributing gloves to everyone. He told Calvin and Benjamin to check the kitchen, den, bathrooms, dining and living rooms. He would check the attic and Erica would check Nina's room. They finished searching those areas and met back in the dining room. With nothing to report, they studied the basement floor plan.

"There are four rooms in the basement: the laundry room, entertainment room, bathroom, and a mini kitchen." Benjamin described the rooms as he remembered them.

"I still get the feeling we're missing something." Erica said.

"I don't know what it could be, Erica. Maybe this is a wild goose chase." Benjamin replied.

"Well, let's go down there and see if anything is out of place. I'm convinced the answers we need are in this house." Erica turned and headed toward the basement, and the others followed.

In the basement, Benjamin led them through each room, but nothing was out of place. As they were about to head back upstairs, a chill ran down Erica's back. In the corner behind the bathroom, she saw a door that was a little smaller than the bathroom entrance.

"Ben, where does that door lead to?" Erica pointed towards the smaller door.

"Oh, I forgot about that room. It's a panic room, but it's never been used to my knowledge."

Erica asked Benjamin to take Calvin upstairs. Once they were gone she turned to Randy.

"This is it, Randy. I sent them upstairs because I don't know what's in that room, but my gut tells me it holds the answers we need." Erica said.

"Okay. Let's proceed." Randy took the lead and walked slowly toward the door. They both had their weapons drawn. Randy twisted the knob, but it didn't budge. He tried again with the same results. All of a sudden, the knob turned from the other side of the door. Randy motioned for Erica to step back. A small gap opened in the door, and a voice whispered.

"Nina, is that you?"

Randy and Erica didn't say a word. The person on the other side of the door opened it a little wider. A woman peek her head out and then walked out the door. She was the spitting image of JJ.

"What's going on?" The lady shrieked. She even sounded like JJ.

"Who are you?" Erica asked the JJ look alike.

"I'm Janice."

"What are you doing here?" Erica spoke calmly.

"Where is Nina?" Janice asked.

"What are you doing here, Janice?" Randy repeated Erica's question.

"I'm not talking to you until I see Nina."

"You don't have a choice." Randy pulled his badge out and Janice eyes widened.

She raised her hands in the air. "I didn't do anything. Where's Nina?"

"Nina isn't here right now. How long have you been down here, Janice?" Randy wanted to keep the situation under control.

"A while, I'm not exactly sure. Why are the police here?"

"We're working on a missing child case." Erica didn't want to give Janice too much information. She couldn't get over how much Janice looked like JJ.

"What does that have to do with Nina?"

"We think Nina is involved." Again Erica was careful with her words.

"She just wanted to save the baby. She shouldn't get in trouble for protecting an innocent child from his abusive father." Janice said in a stronger voice.

"What are you talking about Janice? Do you know where the child is?"

"Yes, but I can't talk to you until I see Nina."

167

"Where is the child, Janice? Do you want to be charged as an accessory to a crime?" Randy said in a stern voice.

"No." Janice shook her head. "But, will you be able to protect him from his dad?"

"What did Nina tell you about the child?" Erica asked.

"She said the baby's mom was in the hospital fighting for her life because her abusive husband beat her badly, and he would do the same to the baby if we didn't keep him safe."

"How did you meet Nina?" Erica asked.

Janice hung her head and lowered her arms. "On the streets, I was homeless. One day, Nina showed up and put me up in a motel. She brought me clothes and fed me food and snacks. Then she told me she needed my help with a sensitive matter and explained why I had to go to that daycare and pick the baby up before his dad went there to get him."

"What is the baby's name? How old is he?" Erica knew she needed to get the whole story out of Janice.

"His name is Leo, and he's about a month old."

"Where is the baby, Janice?" Erica asked.

"He's in the other room asleep."

Erica couldn't wait any longer. She brushed past Janice and ran into the other room while Randy kept his revolver trained on Janice.

"Don't you move." Randy said.

Erica walked over to the baby crib where Leo slept peacefully. With tears in her eyes, she pulled out her cell phone.

After JJ's hello, Erica quickly said. "Hey, I'm on my way. Make sure Lewis is with you." She ended the call before JJ had time to question her. Erica picked up Leo and placed him in the car seat she'd retrieved from the corner of the room. She headed upstairs.

Benjamin called Nathan and told him to bring Nina home.

Chapter Twenty-One

JJ was sitting on the edge of her seat waiting for Erica to arrive. Lewis tried to get her to eat something, but she couldn't. She prayed Erica had a break in the case because she was about to lose her mind. It had been weeks since they saw their son and wondering if he was safe was eating her and Lewis inside out. There was a knock on their front door, and they both jumped. Lewis opened the door.

"Erica, is there any news yet?" JJ was praying Erica had a new lead.

"Yes, JJ, a lot has happened since this morning." Erica went over and hugged Lewis and JJ with tears in her eyes. "I love both of you. May God always bless you and your family."

Now Lewis and JJ were crying. But the next thing they heard and saw made them stop in their tracks. Calvin stood in their living room holding Leo in his arms. The couple was so shocked they just stood there. Then they charged over to Calvin, and he handed Leo to JJ. JJ and Lewis sat on the couch with their baby. All three of them were crying. Erica and

Calvin allowed the couple some time to get reacquainted with their son while they explained what happened with Leo.

"I knew she had him. If I wasn't so happy to have my baby back, I'd go over there and choke the hell out of that crazy heifer." JJ said.

"Sis, I'm going to leave you here with JJ and Lewis. I want to get that ugly van back to the police station and then I'll go fill the rest of the family in on the latest events. Can you find a way back?" Calvin asked Erica.

Erica said she was good, and Calvin said good-bye to JJ and Lewis. Lewis walked Calvin to the door and Erica continued the story.

"JJ, all of this was surreal. Janice thought she was protecting Leo and it was hard for us to convince her to tell us where they were holding him."

"How could she do this Erica? She had to know something wasn't right with Nina's story."

"No, JJ. She thought Nina was doing a heroic thing protecting Leo."

"Does she really look that much like me Erica?"

"Yes, and she actually sounds a lot like you too. I'm sure she has been filled in on the entire story by now. Do you think you're ready to meet her?"

"I don't know. It looks like she took great care of Leo, but all I can think about is never letting my baby out of my sight. I won't be back to work until we can set up child-care on-site.
I'll never let something like this happen to my baby again."

"I wonder what Nina's final plan was. Janice said Nina promised her she would be able to go and live her life in a few days, so I know she had something up her sleeve."

"Well, this time she's not getting off the hook. I'm going to make sure she's prosecuted to the fullest extent of the law." JJ said angrily.

"JJ, I know you haven't had time to think about it, but Janice was just a pawn in Nina's game. You aren't planning on bringing charges against her, are you?"

"I don't know. I have to talk to Lewis and interview her myself before I can make that decision."

"We know the hard life she had. Nina totally manipulated her."

172

"I know it seems like that, but how could she believe everything Nina told her?"

"I don't know, JJ. I think Nina can be pretty convincing when she puts her mind to it. Besides, Janice is the family you talked about for so long. Wouldn't it be nice to have a family member you could be close to? Look at how well she took care of Leo. All of this is going to be hard and overwhelming for her because she was hurting you without realizing it."

"Can we talk about this more tomorrow? I just want to spend some quiet time with my husband and son."

"Sure we can. I have to go check on my bunch of munchkins anyway." Erica gave JJ a hug and left to call a cab.

On the other side of town Randy and Benjamin sat in Nathan's living room waiting on Nathan to bring Nina home. Randy further interrogated Janice and concluded she had no idea what Nina was planning. He felt sorry for Janice and noticed right off the bat she looked identical to JJ, but she didn't have JJ's strength or confidence. She didn't know the entire story of how Nina used her in her plot to get revenge on JJ. He told her to pack her things and wait upstairs in Nina's bedroom until someone came to get her. Janice had looked around the house and saw how spacious and nice it was. She wondered aloud why Nina kept her and Leo in that small room, but Randy wouldn't answer any of her questions. He told her once Nina arrived they would talk more.

"Chief Williamson, what's going to happen to Nina?" Benjamin asked.

"She's going to be arrested on several charges, the most severe being kidnapping."

"What kind of time is she looking at?"

"If convicted, the crime of kidnapping carries a fifty thousand dollar fine and imprisonment up to life."

"Wow. This is going to destroy Nathan and the children." Benjamin lamented.

"There are a lot of factors to be considered. We'll just have to wait and see. There may be charges for what she did to Janice also." Randy stopped talking when he heard Nathan and Nina enter the house. He could hear Nina talking happily to her dad.

Nina walked into the living room and froze.

"What's going on here? I know this is not another one of your games, Ben. I've been going to those stupid classes and therapy sessions as ordered."

"Hi, Nina, no one is playing a game with you." Benjamin said.

"Daddy what's going on here?" Nina turned to her dad.

"Sit down, baby girl. Chief Williamson has some questions to ask you." Nathan instructed.

Reluctantly, Nina took a seat far away from Randy and Benjamin.

"Nina, do you have anything to tell us regarding the disappearance of Leonard Jeffrey Wheeler?" Randy asked.

"No, I don't."

"Are you sure about that?"

"Stop asking me the same question over and over. I already gave you an answered."

"Okay. Nina Kristen Nicholson-Bailey, you're under arrest for the kidnapping of Leonard Jeffrey Wheeler. You have the right to remain silent. If you give up that right whatever you say can and will be used against you in the court of law. You have a right to an attorney, if you can't afford an attorney one will be appointed to you. Do you understand these rights as they have been stated to you?" Randy handcuffed Nina ignoring all the profanity and names she called him.

A police cruiser waited outside. Nathan told Nina not to make a statement until her attorney was present. Randy didn't ride over with the cruiser that carried Nina, opting for a second cruiser to take him and Janice to the station.

Benjamin and Nathan stayed at the house, and Benjamin filled Nathan in on what Nina had been doing.

Nathan shook his head in disbelief. "Wow. How could she pull something of this magnitude off right under our noses?"

"She was able to do it because we refused to accept how sick she is sir." Benjamin said.

176

"Do you think they could put her in an institution instead of prison? She's not going to get help in prison."

"I don't know, sir, but we're going to get through this together. The children are going to need our strength."

"What was she thinking? Did she really think she was going to get away with this?"

"Yes, I think she did." Benjamin waited while Nathan called an attorney to meet them at the police station.

Chapter Twenty-Two

Two days had passed since Leo's return and JJ and Lewis hadn't let him out of their sight. After explaining his dilemma, they were able to see his pediatrician right away. The doctor did a complete examination and pronounced Leo to be in great health. He said Leo had been well cared for and everything was within normal ranges. JJ and Lewis were relieved.

A bathed and diapered Leo now slept in Lewis' arms on the living room sofa while JJ tapped her foot to an anxious rhythm. They were waiting for Erica to arrive with Janice.

JJ was still uncertain about the entire situation. The two women had shared a brief phone conversation. In her head JJ understood how Nina manipulated Janice, but her heart was telling her to be cautious.

Lewis was supportive and told JJ he would back any decision she made, but he was more open minded like Erica in this situation. He reminded JJ how she had wished for extended family after she found out about her adoption, telling her she couldn't get any closer than a twin sister.

178

There was a knock at the door. Too late to change my mind, JJ thought to herself. She took a deep breath and rubbed her sweaty palms on her pants.

Lewis laid Leo in his bassinet and went to open the door. Dumbfounded, he gawked at Janice. The only difference between her and his wife was their hairstyle. Lewis pulled his face together, greeted the ladies and invited them in.

"Janice," Erica said. "This is your twin sister Jasmine Jefferson-Wheeler. Everyone calls her JJ. And JJ, this is your twin sister Janice Louise Hudson."

JJ and Janice shook hands. JJ noticed how shy her sister seemed.

"Hi, Janice, it's nice to meet you." JJ felt strange looking at someone with her face.

"It's nice to meet you too, JJ." Janice stared at JJ for a long time then shyly looked down at the floor. "It's weird looking at someone with my face."

JJ nodded her head. "I know what you mean. Please have a seat." JJ led Janice to the sofa. "I'm sorry it took so long for us to meet, but I needed time alone with Leo." She grabbed Lewis's hand. "We'd like to thank you for taking such good care of our baby."

Lewis nodded. "Ladies, I'm gonna take Leo upstairs and let you talk. Janice it was nice to meet you."

Janice gave Lewis a slight smile and said. "At first, I was so nervous because I haven't been around children much," she continued unable to meet JJ's eye contact. "But, I got the hang of it."

"Do you feel like talking about what happened?" JJ asked.

Before Janice could answer, Erica said she should go so the ladies could get to know each other. The suggestion put a look of fear on Janice's face.

"It's okay, Janice. JJ will take good care of you." Erica tried to reassure Janice.

"Erica, I don't want Janice to feel uncomfortable. Would you be able to stay for a little while?" JJ asked. Truthfully, she was uncomfortable too.

"I'm sorry, JJ." Janice said. "After what happened with Nina, I'm having a problem trusting people. I need to apologize to you. I thought I was saving Leo from his abusive father until his mom was ready to take him back."

"I don't blame you for what happened, Janice. I know how persuasive Nina can be."

"She did so much for me. I thought we were friends. I've never run into somebody like her before. On the streets, we learned to survive and trust each other. I knew she wasn't one of us even though she tried to pass herself off that way."

"What was her plan for Leo?" JJ needed to know what the final phase was in Nina's plan since she wasn't talking.

"I thought it was to give him back to his mom once she got out of the hospital. She said I would be able to leave in a few days and didn't have to worry about Leo."

"Can you tell me a little about yourself? I can tell you what I know and if you're comfortable you can fill in the blanks." JJ offered.

"How did you find out about me?" Janice asked.

"Six months before my adoptive mom passed away, she found out you hadn't died at childbirth and hired a firm to find you. That was about ten years ago."

"So she wanted me?"

"Yes. She was promised both of us, but the broker said you died in childbirth because he was able to get more money separating us."

"A broker? Why was a broker involved?"

"My parents couldn't go through a normal adoption because my dad had a criminal record."

"Oh. You were lucky they wanted you. My adoptive parents wanted me until they could have a child of their own then they put me in foster care. I was four years old." Janice said.

"My dad died when I was a teenager, but I was so angry when my mom told me about the adoption on her deathbed. They had no intention of ever telling me about it."

"I don't mean to be forward, JJ, but be thankful they loved you enough to raise you and showed you the love and attention every child needs." Janice swiped a tear. "I didn't understand why I felt a connection to Leo. I was apprehensive about taking care of him. But seeing his little face looking at me, I felt something I've never felt before, and all I wanted to do was protect him. I got tired of feeling trapped in that little room, but having Leo there made it bearable."

"Thank you for doing that. My husband and I were going out of our minds wondering if he was being care for properly."

"Do you mind if I take a peep at him before I leave?

"Sure, I'll take you up to see him." Not wanting to place Janice in an uncomfortable environment, JJ turned to Erica. "Do you want to come too?"

Erica shook her head and said she would pass.

JJ and Janice were upstairs about ten minutes and when they returned, Erica and Janice left.

JJ sat in the middle of her living room floor and cried. She had her baby back, and she had a sister.

Nathan sat in the police station lobby with Benjamin waiting to see Nina. Until today, Nina refused to see anyone. Both Nathan and Benjamin stood when Randy came to meet them. Randy took them to his office so they could talk privately.

"Nathan, you need to convince Nina to plead guilty so she won't have to go to trial. Her attorney has counseled her to plead guilty due to temporary insanity, but she's insistent about her innocence. I'm afraid her attitude and lack of remorse for what she did is going to get her a life sentence." Randy didn't sugarcoat the trouble Nina was facing.

"I plan on doing that, but she's so stubborn she would rather go to prison than admit she did something wrong." Nathan said.

"Even at the risk of not being able to see her children again? Prison isn't going to get her the help she needs. Would the report from her therapist support her insanity plea?" Benjamin asked.

"Is she that far gone, Chief Williamson?" Nathan was worried about Nina.

"Nina is a very angry and sick woman. She's blaming everyone but herself for her actions, especially Benjamin and JJ. She won't listen to her attorney even when he told her not to make a statement. She felt she had every right to take Leo because JJ was helping Benjamin take her children away." Randy told them.

"She's definitely not in her right mind. I couldn't believe she told you she was going to sell Leo on the black market. When her attorney told me that, I knew she had lost it. Refusing to see me didn't make matters any better. To think she was going to sell that baby to the highest bidder was beyond insane." Nathan said.

"You have thirty minutes, Nathan. Don't be surprised if she cuts the visit short because she's been all over the place." Randy said. "She's going to be evaluated by the state's therapist later this afternoon. Benjamin, you can wait for Nathan in the lobby while I take him back to see Nina."

The men stood and headed for the door.

Chapter Twenty-Three

Emily and the ladies decided to get together Sunday after church for brunch to continue planning Arlene's upcoming wedding. As usual, Delores was running late. It took a lot of convincing, but they talked Janice into joining them for church and brunch. Janice was still wary around a lot of people, but she had been living with Emily since Nina's arrest and felt comfortable with Erica, Emily, and Erin. The ladies knew she was trying to build a relationship with JJ, but it was going slow. Janice felt guilty for JJ's misery. The more JJ reached out to her, the more Janice pulled back, placing Erica in the middle to play peace-maker.

The group decided to meet at Slows BBQ in downtown Detroit. The upscale restaurant, one of Arlene's favorites, was elegant and classy.

As the ladies placed their drink and appetizer orders, Delores rushed to the table apologizing for being late.

Once Delores had taken a seat, Emily took out her pad and pen and hit the side of her glass to get everyone's attention.

"Thank you all for being here today. As you all know we're set with the church and the reception hall. Now we need to settle on a time to meet for the fittings. Lennie has decided to go with powder blue or off-white for the colors, so the dresses have to be one of those colors."

"I vote for powder blue. I would look dreadful in off-white." Delores was first to cast a vote.

The other ladies said whatever color Arlene preferred was good with them. Arlene went with the powder blue and they ordered their food.

Once they were done with their food, Emily reviewed the plans.

"We need volunteers for the flowers, catering, guest list, photographers/videographer, band/deejay, and invitations."

"Mom, I can do the guest list and invitations. With the way things are at work and home, I don't want to take on too much, but I can handle that. " Erica offered.

"I can take care of the flowers, Emily." Erin volunteered.

"I'll take care of the photographers and videographer." Delores said.

"Ok, ladies, this is good. I can take care of the catering." Emily said.

"The only thing left is the band or deejay. Janice would you like to work on this with JJ?"

"I guess that would work." Janice replied. "But I don't know how to go about booking something like that, Emily."

"Don't worry," Emily said. "JJ will be there to help you." Emily clapped her hands. "Okay, everyone. I think we're good for now."

"Is there anything else you ladies would like to add?"

Everyone shook their heads. Then Janice said softly.

"I really appreciate you all including me in the planning, but I don't even know if I'll be around months from now."

"Why wouldn't you be around, Janice?" Emily didn't like the sad look on Janice's face.

"Can we talk about this later, Emily?" Janice looked like she was close to tears so Emily nodded her head.

"Okay," Emily said, clearing her throat. "If no one has anything else to add, we can set up another meeting next month to see how everything is coming along. I'll reach out to all of you next week with a time and place." Emily ended the meeting and the ladies set off to enjoy the rest of their day.

Emily noticed Janice was still shy around Arlene and Delores and she had been quiet on their ride back from the meeting. She didn't want to force Janice to talk until she was ready. Once they arrived home and were settled into the family room, Emily asked Janice if she felt like talking about what was on her mind.

"Emily, all of you guys have been so nice to me and I don't know why."

"We're nice to you because you're part of our family."

"I don't know how to react to all of this. I'm not use to anyone taking care of me and to tell you the truth after trusting Nina which was a big mistake, I don't want to open myself up again."

"Janice, what Nina did to you was horrible, but she is a very sick woman. I know this may sound crazy, but I think she really cared about you as much as she could. I also know even though she did horrible things, she's not beyond help because she made sure you and Leo had what you guys needed."

"I know and that's why I'm so conflicted. I want to get to know JJ better, but I think what happened with Leo will always come between us. Then on the other hand, I feel like a traitor for not supporting Nina after all she's done for me."

"May I make a suggestion?"

"Sure."

"A few years back, Lennie and I were involved in a dangerous ordeal that almost ended our lives. We ended up getting professional help to work through our issues. My therapist helped me out tremendously. I think she would be able to help you sort through all the conflicting emotions inside of you."

"I don't know if that will work. I have trouble opening up to strangers, Emily. Plus, I don't have insurance or money to see a therapist."

"That's another thing I wanted to talk to you about. How do you feel about going back to work?"

Janice shook her head. "I don't have the means or any idea how to go about getting back out there. Sometimes I feel like I'm afraid of my own shadow."

"You just need to take one step at a time. Will you let Lennie and I help you get back on your feet?"

"I'm a little afraid of talking with Arlene."

"Lennie is hard to warm up to or get to know, but she's a great person. We have known each other since we were eleven years old. Back then I was a shy and withdrawn young girl, but little by little, she gave me the confidence to become my own person. My therapy sessions put the icing on the cake."

"What did you guys have in mind?" Janice was curious.

"We know you're a proud woman and that you don't want any handouts, so I was thinking we could set you up with therapy first. Then when you're ready, you can work for me here out of my home office where you can collect a salary and benefits. Once you're on your feet, you can go to work with Lennie. She could use someone with your background at her company. Plus, you would be in the same building as JJ and Erica so that would give you a chance to work on your relationship with JJ." Emily gave Janice's hands a light squeeze.

"That sounds like it would work." Janice said.

"If that doesn't work out, we could help you find another position. JJ and Erica may have something for you with their company."

"You're right, Emily. I want to be able to pay my own way. I don't know how to rejoin the workforce, but I know it's time for me to do it."

"Would you like me to schedule you an appointment with Dr. Patterson? She was the therapist that helped me."

"Yes, that would be great. What kind of work would I be doing for you? I don't want to be a burden."

"It would be something within your skill set. Accounting/finance or you could come to the office with me and serve as my assistant since I don't know how long Lewis will be out."

"I don't want to step on any toes."

"It's okay, Janice. Lewis is doing the bulk of his work from home. I just thought you might like being in a business environment."

"Is it okay for me to start off with the therapist for a few weeks and then come to the office with you?"

"Sure. We can also pay visits to Lennie's building too, that way she can introduce you to her staff. Her firm may be a better fit for a permanent position when you're ready."

"Emily, I'm kind of worried that you, Erin, and Erica are the only ones I'll ever feel comfortable around. I thought by now I would feel closer to JJ since she's my twin."

"All of this takes time, Janice. Don't worry about that. Dr. Patterson will help you with anything that is bothering you. Before you know it, you'll get over the wariness about Lennie and Delores too. Both women have strong personalities, but they don't bite."

Janice smiled. "Thanks for helping me out. I don't know why I've been blessed with people like you guys, but I know I don't want to mess it up."

"You may want to go and get a little rest before you meet Eric and DJ later this evening.

Eric has taken care of all of us since he was eighteen and we adore him to no end. He was sorry they were out of town while most of this was going on."

"That's your brother and nephew, Delores' husband and son, correct?"

"Yes, that's right." Emily patted Janice's arm. "I think I'll take a short nap too. See you at dinnertime."

Chapter Twenty-Four

Janice and Erica sat in the visiting room waiting to see Nina. Janice was thankful no charges were brought against her for her role in Leo's kidnapping, but she had no idea why Nina wanted to see her. She didn't trust Nina anymore and only agreed to see her with Erica present.

Janice was headed to JJ's house after they left the police station. She had spoken with JJ last night and was happy she agreed to let her come over and visit with Leo. Sometimes she felt overwhelmed with everything that had happened to her since she met Nina. Emily told her she would feel better once she realized how many people cared about her, but Janice wasn't sure about that. Her first appointment with Dr. Patterson was in the morning, and she wondered if therapy would really help.

She had enjoyed meeting Eric and DJ last night and was surprised that she felt at ease with them. Janice was drawn to Eric's positive aura. She wasn't surprised to learn JJ had once loved him. The dinner Emily prepared for them was nice and relaxing until Delores showed up and spoiled the mood. Janice could tell she was the jealous type who didn't want any woman around her husband, so she excused herself a few minutes after Delores arrived.

"Janice. Janice." Erica gently put her hand on Janice's shoulder.

"Are you okay?"

"I'm sorry. I was just wondering why Nina wanted to see me when she banned everyone else except her dad."

"I'm curious about that too."

"I don't know what to say to her or how to feel about the things she's done, Erica."

"You just need time to process everything. Don't rush or get impatient about your feelings."

"It's hard for me to understand why you and your family are being so nice to me."

"You're part of our family now and we always take care of each other. I just can't wait until you get to really know all of us, especially JJ. Your sister is a great person. I know it's weird for both of you right now, but it will change when you guys spend more time together."

"I get the feeling she still blames me a little bit for what happened to Leo, and I don't know how to get around that."

"She doesn't Janice. I know JJ's lack of contact may concern you, but she just wants to spend a little time alone with Leo and Lewis."

"It's not just that, Erica. I find it hard to look at her face and see my own staring back at me. I know it must be the same for her too."

"Yes, it is, but JJ is a strong woman and deep down you are too. You just had a lot of unfortunate events happen in your life that makes it difficult for you to trust people."

"I don't ever remember being a strong person even when Vincent was alive, and that period in my life was the only time I can say I was strong enough to face my life head on."

"Once you start therapy, you'll see that you have been stronger than you think. Just look at all you've overcome."

Nina was escorted into the visiting room in chains and locked down to the table where they were sitting, halting their conversation.

"Hi, Nina, how are you doing?" Erica asked.

Nina ignored Erica and spoke to Janice.

197

"Thank you for coming, Janice."

"I don't know what to say to you, Nina."

"Then don't say anything, just listen please. I was down on my luck and needed a hit when I ran into you. I felt like my whole world was falling apart and there you were. I did a double take because at first I thought you were the person I hated most in the world. Your sister's job forces her to go undercover sometimes so my first thought was to expose her in that crime-ridden neighborhood. After I talked with you for a few minutes and you didn't recognize me, I knew you wasn't that bitch."

"Nina, I'm not going to sit here and let you put JJ down. If you can't keep this civil, we're leaving." Erica said.

"You're not wanted here so don't talk to me." Nina growled.

"Well, I'm here so you're just going to have to deal with it."

"As I was saying, Janice, when you didn't recognize me, I thought you would be useful, so I befriended you and started my plan to pay back the woman that was trying to take my children from me."

"Nina, I trusted you. I thought you cared about me and wanted to help me." Janice said.

"I did come to care for you, Janice. That's why when you became restless, I worked harder to get you the money I promised you and finalize my plan for that poor baby."

"Nina, I'm sorry, but I can't deal with this right now."

"Please, Janice. I just want you to understand that I'm sorry for what I did to you. Outside of my children and dad, there is no one else I care about but you."

"Good luck, Nina." Janice stood and walked out of the room.

"Nina, you really need to plead guilty so you can get help and put everyone out of their misery." Erica said.

"Bitch, I told you not to talk to me. My life is turned upside down because of you and that friend of yours."

"No, Nina. Ben had all of this in motion before we became involved. You are responsible for your life imploding, no one else."

"Guard! Get me out of here. It stinks." Nina yelled.

Janice was in her own world on the way to JJ's. She was happy JJ had called last night and invited her to come hang out with her and Leo. Janice loved Leo and she really did want to get to know her sister better. She even told Erica she would be fine with her not staying. Janice knocked on JJ's door, her first big step in getting her life back in order.

"Hi, Janice, come on in. Leo and I have been waiting on you."

"Hi, JJ. Thanks for inviting me over."

"No problem. I can't tell you how grateful I am that you took such good care of my baby."

"Unbeknownst to me, I was actually taking care of my nephew. I felt a connection to Leo even though I was scared to death of caring for an infant."

JJ and Janice walked into the living room where Leo lay wide awake in his baby bed. Janice asked if she could hold Leo.

"Sure," JJ said. "I'll go make us a snack."

"How was your meeting with the witch lady?" JJ asked when she returned with a tray.

"It was uncomfortable. I don't know how I should feel about the woman that has played such a big role in my life over the past few weeks."

"No disrespect to you, but I hope they throw the book at that crazy heifer and lock her up for a long time."

"I understand how you feel, JJ, but there's another side to Nina that's not all crazy. She fought the demons of not harming me. She told me she had to fight with everything in her not to hurt me because you are the one person in the world she hates beyond any other."

"That's something I don't get. I wasn't even in the picture when she and Ben were going through their divorce. He only came to me a few weeks ago when he saw how self-destructive Nina had become."

"We may never know the answers. I just want to try to rebuild my life and I'm well on my way with Erica and Emily's help."

"Janice, why didn't you come to me for help?"

"I don't know, JJ. It's easy being around Erica and Emily. Their concern for me is genuine. It's easy to open up to them."

"I know what you mean. I felt the same way. How about this? Let's plan on spending more time together and maybe that will be a start. You're even welcome to move in with us if that's what you want to do."

"I'll think about it."

The ladies spent the rest of the day together until Erica came to take Janice back to Emily's house.

Chapter Twenty-Five

Arlene was at the office tying up a few lose ends. She had errands to run before tonight's small dinner party. She adjusted herself in the back seat of her car when it arrived, tapped on the window separating her from the driver and told him to take her to the condo. She didn't have much time before her hair stylist arrived to ready her for tonight's event. Arlene leaned her head against the seat and closed her eyes. It had been a busy week. After several calming breaths, she opened her eyes and realized her driver was going in the wrong direction.

"Ian, I told you to take me to the condo. Ian. Ian?" Arlene became alarmed when the driver kept driving without acknowledging her command. "Ian, turn this car around this instant."

Arlene tapped on the window, but the driver kept going. By the time they came to a stop, Arlene was dialing Eric on her cell phone. The driver hopped out of the car, opened the door and ripped the phone out of Arlene's hand. He pulled her out of the car. Arlene stumbled, recovered and attempted to kick her assailant in the groin. Anticipating the move, her assailant deflected her kick and grabbed her arms, dragging her into a small log cabin. Arlene struggled without success. She awoke handcuffed to a chair, feet and mouth bound with masking tape. The room was dim but not completely dark. A large figure came into focus and Arlene was face-to-face with Dr. Samuel Baker.

"You know I'm not going to hurt you, Arlene. I just wanted to get some private time with you so I could talk some sense into you about your relationship with my brother." Samuel leaned his face in too close for Arlene's comfort.

Arlene was mad as hell. Now she wished she had let Eric take care of this crazy fool.

"I'm going to take the tape off your mouth. We're in a secluded area so your screams will go unheard."

"What the hell is wrong with you, Sam?" Arlene started right in on him as soon as the tape was removed from her mouth. "Why the hell did you bring me out here?"

"Arlene, you were making it difficult for me to get alone time with you, and I have to talk you out of this foolishness. You're not going to marry my brother."

"There is no foolishness going on in my relationship with Cedric. We love each other and we're going to be married in a few months."

"How do you expect me to let that happen with the way I feel about you?"

"Feel about me? Sam, I don't know what the hell you think you feel about me, but I am in love with your brother and we're getting married. You need to accept that and respect our decision. What the hell is wrong with you bringing me out here? You could be arrested for kidnapping and lose your practice."

"That's not going to happen. I love you and I know you feel the same way. We made a connection that can't be broken."

"The only connection we have, Dr. Baker, is that you're related to the man I'm about to marry. Bringing me out here against my will isn't going to accomplish anything. Now take me back home please." Arlene was horrified that Samuel said he loved her. That had come from left field.

"Are you trying to tell me you don't have feelings for me, Arlene?"

"What I feel, Sam, is appreciation for the progress I've made when I went through therapy and brotherly love because you are Cedric's, my future husband's brother. But I do not feel anything romantic towards you.

Sam shook his head. "That can't be true. I know you care about Cedric, but what about what we feel for each other?" Samuel's face held a glazed over expression.

"Sam, please stop this and take me back home."

Sam shook his head again. "Not until you admit you're making a mistake marrying my brother. The two of you hardly have anything in common."

"That's just it, Sam. You know the old saying 'opposites attract', that's who Cedric and I are together."

"You're going to get bored with him within a year, and then what?"

"That's not going to happen. We complement each other in ways you may not understand."

"I have to go. I can't stand back and let you make a fool out of my brother."

Arlene panicked when Samuel turned to leave. He turned at her yelp and reapplied fresh tape to her mouth, leaving Arlene to ponder what he'd said in the dark.

Emily wondered what was keeping Arlene. She was supposed to be there a half hour ago.

She smiled to herself thinking Arlene was probably trying to outdo Delores by pulling a grand entrance like Delores always seemed to do when they met up. Delores had a habit of making sure she was the last to arrive whenever they met. Emily wondered if Delores derived some sense of power from her delayed entrances. She looked over to the corner where Delores and Eric stood sipping their drinks. They were one great looking power couple. Randy came up behind Emily and gave her a big hug.

"How is the prettiest girl in the world doing?" He said into her ear.

"I don't know how she's doing because she's not here." Emily chuckled and turned to her husband. "But I'm going to have a few words with her when she arrives."

"You're mistaken, Emily. You're the prettiest girl I'm talking about." Randy smiled.

"Why thank you, honey. I was sure you meant Lennie. I have no idea what's keeping her. Perhaps she's pulling one of Delores numbers, being late intentionally to make an entrance."

"That sounds like something she'd do to put Delores in her place.

"Well, I just hope she hurries so we can head over to the restaurant." Emily and Randy stopped talking when Eric and Delores joined them.

"Where is Arlene? I'm starving." Delores asked, looking at her watch.

"I'm sure she'll be here shortly. Why don't I go give her a call and see what's keeping her?" Emily excused herself.

"I think it's rude for Arlene to keep us waiting. We should just go and have her meet us at the restaurant." Delores suggested.

"Honey, we arranged to meet here. Give Emily a minute to see what's going on." Eric said.

Worry etched Emily's face when she returned.

"Eric, I couldn't reach Lennie. I hope everything's okay. I'm not sure what to think. Lennie's usually prompt."

"Well, let's not worry just yet. She's not that late. We can give her a little more time." Eric said.

When Cedric called to see why they weren't at the restaurant yet, Emily turned to Randy.

"I don't like this. Can you check to see if there were any accidents or anything reported?"

"Sure honey," he said, giving her hand a gentle squeeze. "but don't get yourself all worked up." Randy left the trio to call the police station.

Eric excused himself from Emily and Delores and called Samuel's office. His assistant told Eric he was with a patient. Eric returned to the group and asked Randy to see the ladies safely to the restaurant, informing them that he needed to make a stop on the way.

Eric arrived at Samuel's office and demanded to see him. Fifteen minutes later, the assistant showed Eric into Samuel's office.

"Hello, Eric. How are you doing this evening?" Samuel had a big smile on his face.

"I'd be better if I was at the restaurant with my family."

"What brings you by?" Samuel asked.

"Arlene was supposed to meet us for drinks at Emily's before going to the restaurant, but she never showed up."

"What does that have to do with why you're in my office?" Samuel asked coolly.

"You have a problem with her engagement to your brother, and you've been giving her a hard time."

"I wouldn't say a hard time, but I do feel they're rushing their relationship. I've told Arlene that. I don't want her to have a setback. She's worked hard to get to where she is today."

"That's not for you to decide, Samuel. That's up to Arlene and Cedric."

"I understand that completely, but I know my brother, and I don't want this relationship to break him."

"Again, that's his decision not yours. You need to stay out of things that do not concern you."

"I know. Arlene made it perfectly clear she didn't want me to interfere in her relationship with Cedric."

"When was the last time you saw my sister?"

"Earlier in the week, I met her and Cedric for dinner."

"I see," Eric nodded. "Thanks for your time, Samuel."

Eric left Samuel's office and drove toward the restaurant. *"He's not telling the truth...I know it."*

Chapter Twenty-Six

Arlene was mad as hell. It felt like a lifetime since Samuel had left her in the dark. She was hungry and she had to use the bathroom. *That foolish man better hurry his ass back here and let me go.* Her family and Cedric had to be worried about her. By now, she should've been sitting at the table enjoying dinner. *I know Delores was complaining about me being late. Humph. That woman is late for everything.* Arlene heard the knob turn on the door and couldn't wait to get that nasty tape off her mouth.

"Honey, I'm home." Samuel had a big smile on his face.

Arlene glared at him.

"What's the matter? You don't look happy to see me, Arlene." He walked over and pulled the tape off quickly.

"Ouch!" Arlene yelped.

"I'm sorry. Did I hurt you?" Samuel frowned.

Arlene ignored his question. "How long do you plan on keeping me here against my will? My mouth is dry. I need to go to the restroom and I need to eat. Cedric and my family are waiting for me at the restaurant."

"You don't have a how was your day or something nice to say to me, honey?"

"Stop calling me that. I'm not your honey."

"Don't act like that. I was hoping you had thought about what I said while I was away."

"Why are you talking to me like this is a normal situation? You have abducted me, handcuffed me to a chair and taped my hands and feet so I can't move. Then you walk in here like we're a couple or something. Take me to the restroom now and then take me home."

"Come on. I'll take you to the restroom."

Samuel unlocked the handcuffs, picked Arlene up and carried her to the bathroom at the back of the small cabin.

"Don't try anything funny, honey. I'm going to release your feet and cuff one hand to the pole so you can use the other hand to take care of your business." He removed the tape from her feet. I'll be standing right outside this door so don't try anything funny, honey." Samuel closed the door as he left the bathroom.

After she finished relieving herself, Arlene looked around for something she could use as a weapon. Before she could find anything, Samuel came back into the bathroom cuffed her hands together and carried her back to the high back chair he had her sitting in while he was away.

"How long are you planning on keeping me here?"

"That depends on you. Are you ready to admit you're wrong about your relationship with my brother and break things off with him?"

"Sam, I've already told you. That's not going to happen, so you need to cut your losses and move on. Let's just chalk this up as a misunderstanding and call it a day."

"Now you think I'm stupid, Arlene. You're not going to talk your way out of this. You've forgotten how well I know you. I'm not going to fall at your feet like the dozens of other men you've had in your life including my clueless big brother."

"Don't talk about him like that, Sam. Cedric is a great man. I'm lucky he wants to spend the rest of his life with me."

"Oh no, don't get me wrong. I love my big brother, but he's always had a blind spot for the wrong woman. Did he tell you his wife wanted to be with me before they got married?"

"Yes, Sam. Cedric told me his wife admitted she was attracted to you, but she was in love with him. Is that what this all about? Women who prefer a construction foreman over the highly acclaimed doctor." Arlene didn't care if she was pissing Samuel off.

"Don't talk to me like that, honey. I know you just need a little bit more time to think about this. I'll go fix you something to eat." Samuel left the room and headed to the kitchen.

Emily was worried when Arlene failed to call or show up at the restaurant. She headed home and called everyone she could think of who would know Arlene's whereabouts. Erica was her first call. "Hi, honey. Do you happen to know what time Lennie left the office today?"

"Hi, Mom, Auntie left around ten thirty, is everything ok?"

"Well, I'm really not sure, sweetie. Lennie was supposed to meet up with the family at my house for drinks before dinner and she didn't show up here or at the restaurant."

"That doesn't sound good, Mom."

"I know. Randy is at the station now to see what he can find out."

"I'll be right over, Mom."

"No don't. I'll keep you posted. Your uncle Eric is here with me."

"Ok, Mom, but I'm only a phone call away if you guys need my help."

"I know, baby girl. I'll talk to you later."

"What time did she leave the office?" Eric asked when Emily returned.

"Erica said it was around ten-thirty."

"I still don't like how cocky Samuel was acting. I'm going to call Cedric and have him check with his brother to see if he can get anything

216

out of him. Before I came to the restaurant, I called her car service to see where the last place they dropped her off. They said they dropped her off at work this morning and she was supposed to let them know what time to pick her up, but she never called them." Eric said.

"What could have happened to her, Eric?" Emily rubbed her hands together.

Shaking his head, Eric went to the family room and called Cedric. Emily walked in just as he placed the phone back on its base. Eric rubbed his hand across his head. "Well, Cedric said he spoke to Samuel and Samuel said he hasn't heard from Arlene."

"Lennie wouldn't just run out on us like that, Eric. I wish Randy would hurry up with some news."

"I don't think we should panic, Emily. There could be a simple explanation as to why she didn't show up for dinner."

"I'm going to let her have it when she does show up. Scaring us like this isn't a responsible thing to do."

Randy returned from the station. "I've checked with the hospitals and no one fitting Arlene's description has been admitted. I also have a few men out patrolling the streets keeping a look out."

In her heart, Emily knew something was wrong. Arlene wouldn't worry them like this without having a good reason.

"I think we should file a missing person's report." Emily said.

"Honey, it's too soon, let's give it a few more hours to see what happens." Randy said.

"I'm going to head home, Emily. Let me know when you hear from Arlene." Eric hugged Emily and shook Randy's hand before leaving.

Chapter Twenty-Seven

Before he pulled away from Emily's house, Eric sat in his car and prayed. He didn't like keeping things from his sister, but his gut told him Arlene was in trouble and Samuel had something to do with it. He called Cedric from his car and told him he would meet him at Arlene's condo. Eric could hear the concern in Cedric's voice. Cedric was proud of his younger brother's accomplishments. It might be hard for him to accept that Samuel would do something to jeopardize his own brother's happiness.

Eric pulled up to Arlene's gated community and punched in her passcode. The guard greeted him as he headed towards her driveway. Months earlier, when Arlene told him she was serious about Cedric, Eric had his doubts. Arlene had been unattached for the longest time since he'd known her, but that was a good thing. She needed time to heal from the mistakes of her past. Eric walked to the door and thought about how he was going to approach Cedric. He could have used his key, but he wanted to respect Cedric's place in Arlene's life and opted to knock on the door instead. Cedric invited him into, and Eric followed him to the living room.

"I guess you still haven't heard anything from Arlene?" Eric could tell by the look on Cedric's face that he hadn't heard from Arlene yet.

"No, I haven't. And I must say, I'm concerned she might be in trouble. There's no way she wouldn't have been in touch with one of us by now."

"That's why I'm here. I know you may not want to accept this, but I think your brother has something to do with Arlene's disappearance." Eric could tell by the look on Cedric's face that he didn't think that was true.

"Why would you think Sammy is involved, Eric?"

"I went to visit him before I met you guys at dinner tonight. He was too cocky about the situation. He also hasn't been shy about expressing that you guys shouldn't be getting married so soon."

"I understand that, Eric, but that doesn't mean he would do something to harm Arlene. My brother has a highly sought after, established psychotherapy practice. He wouldn't do anything to damage his professional credibility. Besides," Cedric said taking a seat on the sofa.

"Sammy knows how important Arlene is to me. The last time we met he even agreed to be my best man."

"What else could he do, say no?" Eric tried to appeal to Cedric. "That wouldn't go over well."

"I think you're wrong. But to be on the safe side I'll give him a call right now to see what he knows."

"Alright, but maybe you should tell him to meet you here or somewhere so you can see his face and body language when you talk to him."

"I'll tell him to come over to my house and I'll be in touch with you as soon as we're done."

"Okay. I'll wait for your call so make sure you get back with me."

Cedric locked Arlene's condo, and he and Eric walked out together headed their separate ways.

Samuel was fed up with Arlene's stubborn behavior. *Why can't she see we're a better fit then she and Cedric?* He knew it didn't have anything to do with the age difference because she was much older than David Jr. when they were dating. He also found it hard to accept that in the long run she would be satisfied in a long-term relationship with his brother. That's why he was pushing her so hard to be with him. They were more compatible professionally and on a personal level. He loved his brother, but he didn't have one adventuresome bone in his body and that's what Arlene was used to getting from men.

Samuel was sitting across from Arlene when Cedric called his cell phone. He hastily taped her mouth and headed to his car to return the call.

"Hi, big brother. My hands were tied. How are you doing?" Frustrated by not getting anywhere with Arlene, Samuel was surprised by his own jovial tone.

"I'm hanging in there. I was wondering if you had time to meet me at my house or someplace convenient. I tried to reach you several times last night, but you were MIA." Cedric said.

"I have a little free time before I dictate some notes for my assistant. You want to meet me at my apartment in say half hour?"

"That's cool, bro. I'll see you then."

Sam hung up the phone and went back into the cabin to let Arlene know he had to leave.

Arlene rolled her eyes and turned her head in the other direction.

Arlene had been fed and Samuel had allowed her to use the restroom, so he knew she would be okay until he could return. He wondered what his brother wanted, but had the feeling it was about Arlene. Samuel figured Eric's nosy ass must have gone crying to Cedric about Arlene being missing. When he arrived at his apartment twenty-five minutes later, Samuel wasn't surprised to see Cedric waiting. The two men entered and went into the living room. Samuel asked Cedric if he wanted anything to drink or eat and Cedric declined.

"What's on your mind, big brother?" Samuel asked.

"I'm worried about Arlene. She's missing. She hasn't been in contact with anyone in over twenty-four hours." Cedric studied Samuel closely to see if he could pick up anything out of the ordinary.

"Man, she probably just cooling her heels somewhere."

Cedric shook his head. "No, she wouldn't go away this long without contacting someone, especially Emily."

"Have you guys filed a missing person's report?"

"Yes, we filed a report a few hours ago, and Randy is putting extra men on the case."

"Seems like you're doing all you can to find her."

"When was the last time you saw or talked to her, Sammy?"

"Now I know what this is about. Eric came to see me yesterday and asked me some questions about Arlene, but he didn't tell me she was missing. He wanted me to stay out of you guys relationship."

"I wouldn't put it that harshly. But you still haven't told me why you feel so strongly about us not being together."

"I know she told you about her past, Cedric. You already know you aren't the type of guy she's used to dealing with on a personal level."

"People change, Sammy. Arlene is older now, and she's been alone for a long time. She's ready for a change."

"I just don't want you to get hurt, Cedric."

"I'm the big brother. I'm supposed to be looking out for you, man."

"You're vulnerable right now, Cedric. Even though you've been a widower for years, this is your first serious relationship since your wife died."

"I know you're concerned about my relationship with Arlene because of her past, and I appreciate you looking out for me. But, I'm telling you, Sammy, you need to get over that. I love her. She loves me and we're going to have a good life together. Just because we come from different backgrounds doesn't mean we can't make this thing work."

Samuel jumped up and started pacing the room.

"You need to face the facts, brother." He yelled at Cedric. "You're not used to being with a woman like Arlene. She's going to get bored with you within a year and go back to her old ways. She needs someone that can handle the fire that runs deep in her veins."

Cedric jumped up. "Is that someone you, Sammy? Is that what this is about? The real reason you've been so against me marrying Arlene. Are you in love with Arlene, little brother?"

Samuel stopped pacing and turned his back to Cedric. "I'm better suited for her than you are, big brother. I know how to handle her fire. You have no idea what to do with that passion."

"Sammy, where is Arlene?"

Samuel turned around. "Why are you asking me where she's at? She's your fiancée. Why would I know where she's at? Isn't it your job to keep up with her? You can handle it, right?

"Please, Sammy. If you know where Arlene is, I need to know right now."

"I already told you. I do not know where she is. Cedric, so stop asking me the same question over and over." Samuel resumed his pacing.

"Sammy, this is eating away at you and it's not healthy."

"Oh, now you want to analyze me, big brother?" Samuel became more agitated.

"No, I want you to tell me what's going on with you and then I want to know what happened to Arlene."

"You want the truth? I'll tell you the truth. I love Arlene. I think she's better off with me, but both of you guys have blinders on and refuse

226

to believe me when I keep telling you your relationship is not going to last." Samuel paced himself into a frenzy.

"Sammy, I need you to calm down. I don't think I've ever seen you like this man." Samuel stopped pacing and sat on the sofa.

"I'm sorry, Cedric." He put his hand on his head. "I shouldn't have dumped all that on you when you're worried about Arlene, but somewhere along the line I fell in love with Arlene.
There isn't any conflict because she's no longer my patient."

"I understand that, but you need to understand that she's going to marry me in a few months, and you need to respect our wishes. Maybe you should take a little time off and go relax on a beach or something."

"Sending me away isn't going to protect your relationship, Cedric."

"I'm not sending you away to protect my relationship. I'm saying you should go away to deal with your feelings. You know it's not healthy to think of Arlene in that way."

"Why, because you guys are the perfect couple and you see me as a threat?"

227

"No, because I'm worried about you, Sammy and what you might have done to Arlene."

"I haven't done anything to Arlene except try to talk her out of making a big mistake by marrying you."

"You know what? I think I'm gonna leave. Please let me know if you hear anything from Arlene." Cedric realized Eric was right, Samuel knew what happened to Arlene, and he would be waiting for Samuel's next move.

Chapter Twenty-Eight

Cedric felt bad about what he was doing to his baby brother, but if keeping an eye on Samuel's movements was the only way to find out what happened to Arlene then that's what he was going to do. It took Cedric about twenty minutes to talk Eric out of assisting in his surveillance. Two hours had passed since Cedric left Samuel's apartment. He figured if Samuel was holding Arlene somewhere, he would be checking on her soon. Shortly after reassuring Eric he would keep him posted, Cedric saw Samuel head toward his car. Samuel looked around like he was making sure no one was watching him. Cedric hoped he didn't mess this up because he felt like this would be his only chance to find Arlene.

Samuel pulled out of his parking space and drove slowly. Cedric made sure he stayed at least two cars behind Samuel. He wished he had access to a different vehicle. If Samuel spotted his Lincoln Town Car, Cedric knew his brother would lead him on a wild goose chase. Three cars separated Cedric from Samuel, who continued to drive in a non-hurried fashion. Twenty minutes of driving led them into a secluded area. Cedric wondered where the hell his brother was going and how he would remain hidden when there were hardly any other cars around.

Samuel slowed and turned down a dimly lit road. The car that separated Cedric from Samuel drove on. Cedric stopped near the corner of the street Samuel turned down. He guessed Samuel felt safer because the taillights on his car moved away at a faster pace before turning into a driveway. The twists and turns Samuel had taken would make it difficult for Cedric to remember how to get back to the main road.

Cedric waited until he felt it was safe enough to walk to where he'd seen Samuel's taillights pull into the driveway. He started down the path, and then returned to get his tire iron. Cedric reached Samuel's car and checked the doors to see if they were locked. Satisfied no one was in the car, he cautiously approached the door of the cabin and squatted to avoid being seen. He could see a dim light through the bottom of the door. Cedric stood a little straighter, but was surprised when he was pushed from behind. The cabin door opened, and Cedric was shoved further inside, accidentally dropping his tire iron. Cedric whirled around and came face-to-face with his angry brother. Before he could say anything, Samuel grabbed him by the arm and shoved him. Cedric was shocked to see Arlene sitting in a chair in the middle of the cabin with her feet bound, hands cuffed behind her back, and mouth covered with masking tape. In a panic, he ran over to Arlene, pulled the tape off her mouth and checked for a pulse. When he found one, he turned to his brother and hit him so hard Samuel fell back. Before Cedric could hit him again, Samuel pulled out a forty-five caliber pistol and told Cedric to back up.

"What the hell have you done, Sammy?" Cedric was furious.

"Why did you follow me here, big brother? You should have let this play out."

"Let what play out? You straight up lied to me. What did you do to her?"

"Nothing, I just needed a little more time to convince her that she needed to be with me instead of you. She is so damn stubborn, she wouldn't budge. She had the nerve to tell me hell would freeze over before she lied to me about what she was feeling. All I needed to hear was that she cared about me too.

"What was your end game? You wouldn't have gotten away with holding her forever."

"Stop asking me all these damn questions, man. I'm trying to think."

Cedric retrieved the pocket knife from his pants and kneeled in front of Arlene. He asked Samuel for the key to the handcuffs. When he didn't get a response, he turned to his brother who now had the gun pointed to his head.

Cedric stood abruptly. "Sammy, please…Let me have the gun."

"Why? I won't have a life after all this is over."

"Yes, you will. I will make sure you get help."

"No, you won't because she won't let you."

"Sammy, I swear on Mom and Dad's graves, I won't let you go through this alone. Please don't leave me. You're the only family I have left."

"The keys are behind you in the back of the desk." Samuel said in a defeated voice.

Cedric turned to look at the desk and then turned back to get the gun away from Samuel. The front door was kicked in with such force it crashed violently against the wall. Randy and two uniformed officers entered the cabin with their guns drawn.

Without thinking, Cedric ran to Samuel and attempted to knock the gun out of his hand. The gun went off. Cedric heard Arlene scream, and then everything went black.

Hours after the incident in the cabin, Arlene was still mad. She couldn't believe Cedric had risked his life for his crazy brother. On top of that, he wanted Arlene to forgive Samuel for what he did to her so he could be treated at a facility instead of going to prison.

Arlene was ready to leave the hospital, but they wanted to keep her for observation and ensure her wrists didn't get infected. Arlene had rubbed them raw trying to get free of the cuffs.

Cedric had been treated and released. Thankfully, the bullet only grazed his head. Samuel was in lockup at the Oakland County Jail. Cedric got in touch with the attorney Samuel had on retainer to represent Samuel at his preliminary hearing.

Arlene was so full of her own thoughts she didn't hear anything Emily said until she heard Samuel's name.

"Don't mention that damn fool to me again, Em. Cedric has a lot of nerve asking me to cut that man some slack."

"Lennie, you have to understand. That's the only family he has left. He loves his brother."

"Well, he's supposed to love me too. Where do I fit into his equation of helping that head case ease out of his charges? You see where that got JJ being nice to Nina. She almost lost her baby."

"Lennie, Samuel's case is different from Nina's. He wasn't trying to hurt you."

"Well, he did, and he needs to pay for his crimes."

"At what cost? Do you really expect Cedric to turn his back on his brother completely?

Would you be able to do that to Eric or anyone else in our family?"

"That's different, Em."

"Yeah, in what way is it different, my dear friend?" Emily leaned down and kissed Arlene on the forehead. "I'm going to check on your discharge papers. Rest your eyes, and I'll be back in a few minutes."

Epilogue

Erica sat in the busy room where everyone was changing out of their wedding attire to the clothes they would wear to Arlene's reception. She couldn't believe this day had finally arrived after all they had been through. Thanksgiving had always been a special day for her family, which is why Arlene chose the Saturday after Thanksgiving to get married. She thought back to Labor Day.

Erica and her family were at Emily's house celebrating Labor Day, along with the rest of the family. A lot had happened over the last few months since Erica and JJ took on Ben's case. Erica had looked around her mom's massive grounds where everyone was enjoying good food and entertainment. They all were resting a lot easier knowing Nina was finally committed to a mental facility in Battle Creek. Nina had admitted she was going to put Leo up for adoption because he deserved a mom better than JJ, but she could never explain how her hatred for JJ began. JJ thought Nina got off easy since she wouldn't be spending any time in jail.

Benjamin received his divorced and full custody of his children. The children had returned home from summer camp two weeks ago.

Nathan sold his house and moved into a spacious three-bedroom apartment in Battle Creek so he could be close to Nina.

To everyone's surprise, Benjamin and Janice started dating. They were taking it slow, but their romance was off to a good start. JJ was happy for her sister because she thought Janice was getting a little too attached to Leo. The relationship between the ladies was much better. It was amazing to see how far Janice had blossom from shy and insecure to self-confident and independent.

A month after visiting Nina in jail, Janice moved into a two-bedroom apartment near Arlene's building where she was working full-time in the finance department. She was still in therapy, but she was making progress coping with her past. Janice was surprised when JJ gave her a cashier's check for her portion of Lucille's will. Erica had watched the two ladies as they sat laughing and joking with each other. She was so happy for them. JJ was back to work full-time now that she used part of their first-floor space as a day-care facility. She was serious about keeping Leo close to her. Lewis was also back to work full-time which made Emily very happy.

Erica left her thoughts with a smile, ringing the bell that was on the dressing table to get everyone's attention. She wanted to make an announcement and give anyone that wanted to say something an opportunity to do so.

She looked around the room with a big smile on her face, happy to be surrounded by so many people who had filled their hearts with love and forgiveness.

"Auntie Arlene, I'm so happy for you. Words cannot express how much you mean to me and the family. You've been there for me all my life. On this very special day in your life, may God make every day as joyous for you as you are today. Mom, you're my rock. I hope I can do for my children what you have done for me. The strength, love, understanding, and patience you've always given me will never be forgotten." Erica gestured with her hand, as if she were parting the crowd. "Okay, everyone now is the time to say whatever is on your mind, but remember to include some special words for Auntie Arlene."

Emily went first.

"Lennie, we've been thick as thieves since we were eleven. You've shown me how little blood means when it comes to family. You're my sister as much as Erin, and I will never regret saying you are the best friend anyone could ever have in a lifetime."

Erin stood.

"Arlene, I spent so many of my younger years resenting you for trying to take my place in Emily's life, until I opened my eyes to see why you were so important to her. May you have God's ever-loving blessing for the rest of your life. You deserve it."

Delores cleared her throat.

"Arlene, we got off to a bad start. Thank you for the talks of encouragement and most of all, thank you for finding your own man. Now that you're off the market, I can finally rest knowing I don't have to worry about you coming after Eric. To the rest of the family and friends, and most importantly Erica, I will always cherish being a part of this wonderful family."

Another friend of the family spoke then JJ yelled it was her turn.

"What can I say, Arlene? You are a firecracker, lady. I'm so glad you didn't set your sights on my man because I don't ever want to have to go up against you. May your life be filled with all the love and joy you can withstand. To my sister Janice, I don't know how I managed without you. Thanks for coming into my life. My dear friend Erica, the mold was broken with you. I couldn't have asked for a better partner and friend. May our business continue to grow and may we never have to deal with any more nutcases." Everyone chuckled.

Erica was about to make the closing statement when Janice asked if she could say something.

"Arlene, thanks for taking a chance on me by giving me a job. I've learned so much from you. Emily, thanks for taking me into your lovely home and putting me on a path to healing. Erica, I feel like you saved my life and I owe you a big thank you for that. Always stay sweet and strong. And last but not least," Janice turned and looked at JJ. Erica smiled at the obvious closeness between JJ and Janice. If you didn't know their story, you would have thought they had grown up together all their lives instead of just finding each other less than six months ago. "Baby sister, I know we are only four minutes apart, but I feel a great deal of responsibility towards you. Having you, Leo, and Lewis as part of my family is a blessing I thought I would never experience. I love you." JJ and Janice embraced.

Erica gathered everyone around in a circle and said a closing prayer before they all headed to the reception hall to get the party started.

Questions

Listed below are some potential questions that can be used for a book club discussion:

Story/Characters

1. What scene in the book was the most pivotal? Would it have made a difference if the scene wasn't in the book?

2. Have you ever been put into a position where you had to forgive someone that has done you wrong? If yes, how did that make you feel?

3. Were there any surprises in the book that stood out? If yes, what were they?

4. Were you able to guess what happened next in any of the storylines?

5. Do you feel that JJ and Erica should have dropped Benjamin's case once their lives started to spiral out of control? Why or why not?

6. Was it hard to relate to Nina's character? Why or why not?

7. Was there any point in the book where you disagreed with one of the character's choices? If yes, what would you have done differently?

8. Did you see a big change in any of the characters by the end of this book?

9. What do you see in store for the main character in this book?

10. Do you think this book should end where it ended, or would you like to have seen something different?

Overall

1. Have you read any other books by Diana Carter? If yes, how were they compared to this book?

2. What if anything did you learn or take away from this book?

3. Did you have any preconceptions about this book before you read it?

4. As you read the book, did your opinion change? If so, how?

5. What would you like to see this author do next?

6. How would you rate the author's overall storytelling abilities?

Back Cover

Deciding that she needed a change in her life, Erica Nicole Blackstone-Clark decided to take her career in a different direction. Teaming up with JJ, Jasmine Jefferson they formed Jefferson and Blackstone Investigations (aka JBI). Their caseload was running smoothly until JJ decided to take on her friend's divorce/child custody case. From the very beginning Erica and JJ's personal and professional lives spiral out of control. Their new client, bank president Benjamin Joseph Bailey hires JBI to investigate his wife Nina to obtain evidence to win his petition for full custody of their two children. There is no end to the havoc Nina creates, from petty incidents to capital crimes, to ensure she receives custody of her children.

Erica's family isn't fairing much better. Erica's aunt deals with an interfering family member that isn't willing to accept her upcoming wedding. Will the danger surrounding her new case and family issues push Erica to a breaking point, or will she find a way to overcome the tremendous obstacles that come her way?

Author Bio

Diana Carter obtained her Master of Management degree from University of Phoenix and is currently working on her DBA in Organizational Leadership at Walden University. She is the author of the three book **Broken Promises** series and stand-alone title *Dark Revenge: The Trey Taylor Story*. She lives in the metropolitan Detroit area.

www.ingramcontent.com/pod-product-compliance
Lightning Source LLC
Chambersburg PA
CBHW021009120726
47905CB00009B/2922